SOM

FOLK
TALES

SOMERSET
FOLK TALES

SHARON JACKSTIES

The History Press

For Joe who has always said that I could and should,
and for Jem who has lived with the consequences
For Di and Dave, and their warm Somerset welcome
For my sister Debbie, without whose expertise and
boundless generosity this would not have been possible

First published 2012

The History Press
The Mill, Brimscombe Port
Stroud, Gloucestershire, GL5 2QG
www.thehistorypress.co.uk

British Library Cataloguing in Publication Data.
A catalogue record for this book is available from the British Library.

ISBN 978 0 7524 6333 9

Typesetting and origination by The History Press
Printed in Great Britain
Manufacturing managed by Jellyfish Print Solutions Ltd

CONTENTS

ACKNOWLEDGEMENTS

My thanks to the following:

Jem Dick, illustrator; Paul James and Mary 'Biddy' Rhodes, Halsway Manor; Kennedy-Grant Memorial Library, Halsway Manor; Les Davies, ranger; Pete Castle, storyteller, musician; Harry Giles, acting divisional engineer, Somerset River Board; Les Cloutman, naturalist and ancient archaeologist; The Langport Ladies' Circle; Langport Senior Citizens' Club; Langport Library Staff; Becky Wright; Eli's (aka the Rose and Crown) Huish Episcopi; Gail Cornell, astronomer and writer; and Diane Shepherd.

INTRODUCTION

Somerset is my adopted county, and being an incomer has given me the privilege of seeing it with new eyes. Although I have lived here for nine years, the familiar has never yet become invisible, and not a day passes without my continuing to notice the beauty and variety of its scenery.

Having been a professional storyteller for more than twenty years, I was naturally eager to make an in-depth study of Somerset's stories. Part of this process involved distinguishing those that were shared with other places from those which this county could claim exclusively as its own. The more I looked and listened, the more aware I became of the huge role that the landscape has played in shaping this county's traditional stories.

My work with local groups, especially amongst the older people of the region, reinforced my fascination with the links between the traditional and mostly anonymous stories of the past, and the living present. Often the theme of a traditional tale would unlock the tongues and memories of the listeners, and I soon noticed that place was as important a trigger as subject matter.

Their joy at being listened to, and the generosity with which they shared stories – personal, family, regional, folk and legendary – inspired me, by nature and training an oral practitioner, to write this book.

This generosity has been mirrored at Halsway Manor, the National Centre for the Folk Arts; this residential centre, in the heart of the Quantock Hills, owns an extensive archive of Ruth Tongue's manuscripts – one of the most important collections of local stories, songs and folklore in the country. The centre gave me unrestricted access to their library and permission to reproduce her work, some of which has not been generally available before.

If I am able to repay all those local people who have supported me, by reminding them of tales half-forgotten or by being in some small way an exponent of our heritage, I shall be more than happy to bear any retribution meted out by historians, archaeologists and naturalists!

As the idea of this book took hold, I began to realise that, of all the counties in England, Somerset boasted the widest range of landscapes; later, I discovered that Ruth Tongue had reached the same conclusion:

> Rivers and rhines and cleeves and mines
> Heather, beech and Severn shale
> Cob and thatch where summer shines
> Open headland to have the gale …
> Somerset bred and Somerset born
> Children of oak and ash and thorn …
> Somerset born and Somerset bred
> Cave and swallet and withy bed
> Meadows a-bloom and orchards a-blow
> Shining sea where the tides do flow
> Purple hill for the hunting horn
> Forests of oak and ash and thorn …

This variety has informed the shape of this book, with each chapter being dedicated to a particular landscape. Thus the settings naturally chose the stories, and, had space permitted, there could have been many more.

As I explored plot and place, it became increasingly clear that Somerset offers the unique as well as the extraordinary and the grandiose. Perhaps its most famous landscape feature is the Cheddar Gorge, the deepest in Britain – and how this was formed is described later.

A less well-known example, but just as remarkable, is its 'inland sea', the region we now call the Somerset Levels. Its many rivers empty into the estuary of one of Britain's major waterways, the Severn. This vast inland sea used to cover an area of up to 400 square miles, its depth determined by seasonal rainfall, the distinction between its sweet and salt waters blurred by tidal surges. From north of Glastonbury to south of Ilminster, this formerly flooded landscape has left its legacy in the impossibly smooth contours of the water-rounded hills, which look as though they were shaped by a giant ice cream scoop.

Recent discoveries indicate that, more than 6,000 years ago, this was the first place in the world where people were managing their wetland habitat. Conquering the struggle of land versus water has, over the millennia, given this county the largest area of man-made land in Britain.

The floodwaters still rise along the rivers Axe, Brue, Cary, Huntspill and Parrett as they flow towards the Bristol Channel, whose tidal surges funnel the floods upstream. The name of the tiny village of Hornblotton recalls the villagers' ancient duty of blowing a horn to warn neighbouring settlements that the waters were rising – 'blotton' being a Saxon word meaning 'to blow'.

One of Somerset's major rivers, the Parrett, is tidal as far as Burrowbridge, and used to be navigable (by seagoing vessels) as far as Langport, which disputably boasts England's first money-lending bank. Visitors to this tiny town are proudly told that, until the 1920s, it was possible to buy a ticket for a berth from there to New York.

As I write, there is a sea change in the draining of the Somerset Levels. Conservationists value these unique wetlands and their ability to support plants found rarely elsewhere, for example sundew and butterwort. The Brue Valley supports a habitat where flora such as bog myrtle are like a floating lens on the bog itself, and need water flowing beneath them. Wind pumps have actually been installed to keep the water levels up, which must be a first for this region! The great crane, not seen here for hundreds of years, has been successfully reintroduced, and opinion is divided as to whether to re-instate the beaver ...

Somerset's coastline includes another unique feature – the Bristol Channel – whose peculiarities give rise to enough stories to form their own book. This stretch of water has the second highest tidal range in the world, with variations in depth of almost 50ft. The speed of its incoming tide continues to prove fatal for many unfortunates, drowned whilst trying to outrun it, or stuck fast in its quaking mudflats and quicksands. Nowadays people water-ski or surf the Severn Bore, the rip tide that causes waves of over 6ft to move upstream at 10mph. Few know that the Severn Sea once flooded most of Somerset, after the only tsunami ever recorded in these islands.

Inland, Glastonbury Tor is justly famous as a spiritual centre for both the old pagan religion and Christianity, and legend tells us that it was the site of the first Christian church. Many believe it to have been a magnet for systems of life and belief from even further afield, as the Glastonbury Zodiac testifies. The twelve signs of the zodiac, in their correct order, together with a thirteenth figure (the Great Dog of Langport, guardian of the Underworld) are so large that they cannot be seen – except from above ... Outlined by earthworks, paths, roads, and the boundaries of ancient fields and waterways, the symbols may predate the developing of the landscape along and around their contours.

These Glastonbury Giants – one of the signs is over five miles across – were discovered by Katherine Maltwood in 1927, while she was working on an early Norman-French manuscript, 'The High History of the Holy Grail', written in Glastonbury Abbey; she found that the knights' encounters with beasts and other characters were mirrored by the topography of the area, and the figures it concealed.

Another feature of Somerset is its incomparable native beverage – 'Zummerzet be where they zoider apples grow'. Some would even say that Somerset folk owe their smooth and rounded accent to this ancient, natural sustenance:

> The constant use of this liquor hath been found by long experience to avail much to health and long life, preserving the Drinkers of it in their full strength and vigour even to very old age … eight men who danced a Morris dance, whose age computed together made eight hundred years … were constant cider drinkers.

If the stories in this book inspire the people who live here to appreciate their home even more, I shall be content. And if they prompt others to visit this place where every stone whispers magic, I shall be content.

Sharon Jacksties, 2012

One

THE SALT SEA STRAND
The Bristol Channel

The Bristol Channel is known to be one of the most treacherous stretches of water in Europe. In the great flood of 1607, a huge wave, attributed to a tsunami in the Irish Sea, flooded 200 square miles of land, drowning 3,000 people. Entire villages were washed away, and the flood reached inland as far as Glastonbury.

Many songs refer to the changeable and destructive nature of this channel, which has taken so many lives:

> Now Severn she's wide as the eye can scan
> And she wrecks them under both craft and man
> Singing farewell shore, 'tis Severn no more
> There's none can ride her mighty bore
> When she do rise with a terrible roar
> Singing farewell shore, 'tis Severn no more.
> Oh Severn do shine and she lies still
> And all comes home both safe and well
> Singing welcome shore, 'tis Severn no more

Despite the dangers of these waters, they provide a specialist living for those whose courage is supplemented by local knowledge passed down through the generations. Making the most of this tidal landscape, special wooden sledges were used

1607.
A true report of certaine wonderfull ouerflowings

to skim over the mud, in order to set nets and willow-basket salmon traps.

Following the great autumn tides, October is the best season for hunting conger eels. This sport is known as 'glatting', and the Severn Sea is the only place where this form of hunting developed. Dogs were trained to sniff out the eels' lairs beneath the rocks, only revealed at lowest tides. The eels – aggressive and territorial – would be poked with a stick at least 8ft long until they were enticed from their hideaways to attack their tormentor. The dogs would worry them, whilst a blow to the head with a glathook (a hooked iron rod) would finish them off. Eels weighing 30lb and measuring over 6ft were not uncommon, and were a match for any dog. The glatter would have to be fast and skilful to avoid injury to his faithful companion.

Oh 'tis in October days when the mudflat open lays
We do take our prong and our dogs along
And a-glatting we do go so merry
When October tide is low, 'tis then the congers go
We do take our prong and our dogs along
And a-glatting we do go so merry
We do turn the rocks about and the dogs will pull them out
We do take our prong and our dogs along
And a-glatting we do go so merry

Stories of giant eels abound; they were perhaps the origin for many regional tales of water monsters, such as sea serpents and asrais.

Berrow Sands is a notoriously shifting body of sand, just submerged enough to be completely hidden at low water. Whole wrecks have disappeared into its sandy grave, with entire crews sucked under by quicksands. Small wonder, then, that it was considered to be the lair of a sea monster ...

~ THE MONSTER FISH ~

Not so long ago that we can't remember, there was a monstrous fish that lived near the Berrow Sands. Its mouth was so big, and it had so many huge teeth, that it could splinter whole boats to get at the crews. It devoured the men, with huge conger eels getting the leftovers. These eels, companions to the monster fish, grew so large that they too were a menace – but not if you were in a boat, only if you fell overboard, and then they would get you, several at a time.

Sometimes, if a boat foundered on those sands, it didn't matter how loudly the sailors called for help or how many flares they set off, as it was too dangerous for another boat to approach; they couldn't tell where the sandbank began, and they would get stuck too.

All you could hope for was that the boat wasn't caught by quicksand, or that the incoming tide would lift it off. Mind you, you also had to hope that you were stuck where the water was too shallow for that monster fish to reach the boat. There are sailors who have seen the fish approach but draw no nearer, because the water wasn't deep enough. And, just when they thought they might be saved by the rising tide, that fish has started lashing with its tail, shifting the sands to get the boat near enough for its jaws to reach it. Some say that the worst way to die in this place was when the boat was sinking in the quicksand and the giant eels got to you first. There have been men who have witnessed this from their boats, being unable to get quite close enough to rescue the trapped crew.

Those giant eels used to bark. You could hear them from the shore, and it meant that they and the giant fish were hungry, and everyone knew it was an especially dangerous time to be in a boat.

Well, there was once a very brave fisherman who heard the barking one moonlit night. He set out for the sands all by himself, knowing that it would be too risky to take anyone with him. Sure enough, in the moonlight he could see those eels raising their heads above the water and barking, and then diving down and nudging the boat from beneath. He could have sworn they were pushing it towards the monster fish, because suddenly there it was, right in front of him,

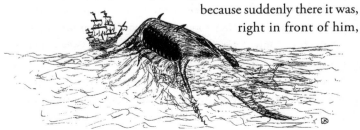

with its huge mouth as big as a cave. It could easily have swallowed the boat whole. The fisherman bided his time until it got close enough, then he took up the anchor chain and he flung that anchor with all his might. It landed in the monster's maw like some giant fish hook, and clean finished him off. Some say it was the cold iron and not the hook that did for him. That fish was never seen again, nor those eels heard to bark.

The Severn coast has its own name for mermaids – sea morgans, who are said to come ashore in St Audries Bay, at the foot of the waterfall which cascades to the beach. Local people call the razor shells found there 'sea morgans' combs'.

~ THE SEA MORGAN'S CHILD ~

There was once an old couple living not far from St Audries. One night the man, who was a fisherman amongst other things, went down towards the beach – but as the tides weren't right for fishing, he must have been about his other business.

It was a calm night, so he could clearly hear singing above the sighing of the surf. It was the most beautiful sound he had ever heard and he yearned to get nearer. Silently he crept closer, until he could plainly see a group of sea morgans on the rocks below the waterfall. Some were dipping in and out of the rock pools, some were combing their long hair with razor shells, and all were singing.

He was so entranced that he stayed listening to them, without noticing that his body had gone stiff with cold. When at last he tried to change his cramped position, he stumbled and alarmed the sea morgans, who had never been so close to a human on the land. In their rush for the water, they left behind one of their children. She was so young that she had not yet started to grow her tail, and she waved her fists and gurgled up at him. The fisherman thought of his own child, who had been buried before she could walk. He scooped up the sea morgan and took her home, where he and his wife doted on her.

If neighbours wondered where she had come from they said nothing, but there was some comment when the couple named her Morgan.

'As though there lacked wholesome Christian names to choose from, and they has to go and choose that heathen-sounding name,' said one of the gossips.

Morgan grew as all children – except that she was overly fond of water and never seemed to feel the cold. She was always paddling through puddles and splashing in streams, and couldn't even pass a bird bath without dabbling and flicking the water. She never seemed to notice if her clothes were sopping wet, whilst her adoptive mother always complained that she could never get her hair dry. But, when she started to sing, the air was filled with such sweetness that no one could stay cross with her; everyone smiled, forgetting her curious ways and their own troubles.

Because of her voice she was wanted in the church choir, but Morgan could never stay in church for long and always slipped away as soon as the service started. One Sunday, the emerging congregation heard splashing and singing, and found her swimming in the millpond. This was too much for the village busybodies, who marched round to her parents' house to complain.

'A gurt girl like that making such a heathen-showing of herself, when she should be at worship like every Christian soul ...' The gossips were trying to bustle into the cottage, whilst the old couple tried to hustle Morgan outside.

'... And if her hair isn't
wringing wet still ...'

Suddenly Morgan cried
out, 'What's that singing?
I know that song!'

Everyone could hear
the most unearthly sweet
sound coming from
the direction of the sea,

and the old man too recognised the song – but pretended he
couldn't hear it.

'They are calling me now – there'll be a storm tonight – they
are calling me with my own song!' And she was gone, running
towards the shore.

The busybodies scuttled off to fetch the priest to chase the
witch away – but they needn't have bothered, because Morgan
was with her own kind as they dived and swam and sang, and
that's where she wanted to stay.

And that night the storm was beyond imagining!

Breakers go crashing to foam as they go
There's laughter and shouting far down below
The ripples they go running all on the incoming tide
Whisper of laughter from side to side
But no one goes looking whoever they may be
No one goes seeking the folk of the sea
The waves all awash on the bars of the beach
Murmur of sorrow, murmur of grief
Now seamen set sail; there's green hair afloat
And eyes under water follow the boat
But no one goes looking whoever they may be
No one goes seeking the folk of the sea

Not all sea morgans were as harmless. One of their loveliest was never seen near the shore, but was heard and seen out to sea. Some say that she fell in love with a sailor and was abandoned by him, and that she had sworn revenge on all of his kind ever since. On moonlit nights, seafarers would hear her singing, and some would even change course to keep that sound with them. Sometimes they were allowed glimpses of her beauty … as she lured them to the lair of a giant eel, who would overturn their boat and devour them.

The sea is the womb
That cradles the grave
That rocks the tomb
That births the wave
That smoothes the bed
That lays the dead

~ Big Blue Ben ~

Big Ben was a huge dragon who lived inland before he became blue. His huge size was matched by his ferocity and he spouted massive quantities of fire. These attributes were coveted by the Devil, who, consumed with envy, wanted Ben for himself – rather like the 'must have' chihuahua that matches a fashion junkie's handbag.

However, those who do not own a mortal soul are less vulnerable to the Devil's inducements and persuasions, and it was some time before they could come to a mutually agreeable arrangement. After some stiff negotiation, it was decided that Ben would draw the Devil's chariot whenever there was an inspection of his ever-expanding kingdom. In return, Ben would be allowed to eat as many of Hell's chargrilled inhabitants as he liked.

This worked well for a time, until the day came when, after some earthly cataclysm, the Devil had to entertain an extra influx of guests. The flames of Hell were fanned to greater heights to accommodate the newcomers, and Ben rushed hither and thither impressing the new arrivals as the Devil showed them to their quarters.

What with the lavish Smaug's Board* (or smorgasbord) of tasty snacks and Hell's extra warm welcome, Ben got too hot and flew away to the coast at Kilve to cool off in the sea. The ensuing billows of steam created such a dense fog that ships were lost and farmers couldn't find their way to their own barns.

Sadly for Ben, he had chosen to refresh himself when the tide happened to be going out. He stuck fast in the mud, partly because his recent gluttony had made him even heavier than usual. When the tide came back in, Ben was drowned, and when it went out again his body was covered with a layer of blue-grey mud. This was made from eroded 'blue lias', a predominant stone in Somerset which can be rather soft and friable. It took days for the fog to disperse and days for the heat from Ben's corpse to subside. With each mud-bearing tide his body acquired another coating, the mud hardening back to its original stony state, baked by the still-raging heat from the dragon's corpse.

As the fog finally cleared, locals discovered their very own naturally created stone dragon. He who had been petrifying was now petrified, and the renamed 'Blue Ben' became the inspiration for the many dragons carved by stonemasons on Somerset's churches.

*as in *The Hobbit* by J.R.R. Tolkien!

A risky and widespread occupation was that of smuggling, which was often the main source of income for those living along Exmoor's coast, an impoverished region due to its poor soil and inaccessible slopes. The little harbour town of Watchet, in particular, was riddled with underground passages for hiding and transporting contraband.

The Severn Sea also brought another hazard, even to those who never left the shore. Piracy has been recorded since the Dark Ages, and was practised as recently as the nineteenth century. The Irish and the Danish used the rivers as gateways to plunder inland, and, as they were also slavers, their most precious booty was man. In later times there were notorious autocrats amongst the pirates – individuals whose crew lived in fear of them and who would prey on anyone.

It was a rare event when any of these murderous tyrants got their comeuppance, and of course by then it was far too late for the many lives which had been destroyed. Yet the stalwart town of Watchet has provided, over the course of its 1,000-year history, many a valiant pirate and ghost-defeating hero.

Far out in the Bristol Channel, lashed by Atlantic storms, lies the small island of Lundy. Now a haven for nature-lovers and those seeking quiet and solitude, its history includes horrific episodes of violence and suffering.

Perhaps its most heartbreaking episode was when it was used to abandon countless transportees bound for the plantations of America, convicts sent to the new colonies to work out their sentences. Such were the difficulties and expense of the Atlantic crossing, let alone the rigours of their working conditions, that they were never expected to be heard of or seen again. None knew this better than the ship's captain; paid to transport them, he would realise that it was far more profitable to never make the voyage at all. So the unfortunate human cargo was frequently marooned on Lundy Island to perish from thirst, hunger and exposure.

~ LOCAL HERO CAPTURES SLAVERS ~

The island was the stronghold of a notorious pirate called Salkeld. There he lived like a king with a small entourage of armed men – all villains themselves, but who were nevertheless terrified of their chief. However, Salkeld afforded them some kind of protection as they were all wanted men, and their situation was considerably better than that of the other inhabitants on the island.

These were captured sailors, whose merchant ships had been seized as they navigated the vital trade route of the Bristol Channel. They were kept as slaves, half-starved and living in appalling conditions; they were helpless victims, until Salkeld made the mistake of capturing George Eskott's boat …

George Eskott was a brave and wily mariner from Watchet, who had endured many hardships and was about to meet his greatest test. He was horrified at what he found when he and his crew were forced in with the other slaves. He couldn't understand how so many could be kept subdued by so few, but months of debilitating conditions had sapped their morale, and being unarmed they had not dared to attack their captors.

Eskott's boat had been bound for Bridgwater with a cargo that included some very potent brandy. This, he guessed, would soon be consumed by Salkeld and his entourage. With his loyal crew, Eskott decided that he would seize the chance of overcoming the pirates if they drank enough to be incapable of defending themselves. This plan gave the others hope, and they waited to see what would happen.

Sounds of merriment clearly indicated that the casks of brandy had been broached. Raucous singing and shouting soon followed, giving way during the night to swearing and brawling. When it grew quieter, Eskott crept nearer to find Salkeld's men dead drunk or staggering. He summoned the other prisoners, and, armed only with a spade, he and his desperate companions attacked, meeting little effective resistance. Now that they were armed with their enemy's weapons, there was little to fear.

Salkeld alone tried to put up a real fight, although he too was very drunk and in no fit state to defend himself. Although Eskott could have finished him off, he gave the pirate chief the chance to surrender. But, knowing the fate that awaited him, Salkeld fought on despite the odds, only to be overpowered and tied up along with the other pirates.

Eskott sailed back to Watchet with a cargo of prisoners and a jubilant crowd of innocent sailors who had thought they would never set foot on the mainland again. The pirates were handed over to the authorities and hanged in due course. Eskott received a hero's welcome; his bravery and cunning were rewarded by King James I himself, who gave him a generous pension.

> Oh Nanny, Oh Nanny I'm frightened,
> Oh Nanny, Oh Nanny I'm scared;
> They say that a bad one is coming
> Who wears a gurt black beard
> He sails his ship over the ocean,
> He sails his ship over the sea;
> And all for to catch pretty maidens

And now he is coming for me.
He carries them over the ocean,
They never see home any more.
He marries or sells or drowns them,
And now he is coming ashore
Go fetch me my father and brothers,
With guns and proud array.
And send for my gallant young sweetheart
To drive Blackbeard away

⤛ THE LAYING OF LUCOTT ⤜

It is no easy task to subdue a malevolent ghost – particularly if it proves resistant to all the usual methods, including exorcism. Some say that Lucott was a smuggler, and others that he was a pirate. What is certain is that he was a vengeful and vicious man, and most were too frightened to mention him at all, whether he was alive or dead.

A week after his burial, his ghost appeared and set about tormenting the inhabitants of Porlock and the surrounding area. This ghost didn't seem subject to the restrictions that might have been expected from an entity that no longer had a physical body. His presence was as corporeal as his malice was far-reaching, but, now that he was dead, he had no fear of capture or punishment. His threats and antics were a shame to the community and the local priest needed no persuading to perform a ceremony of exorcism. This had no effect, except to provoke Lucott's ghost to greater feats of depravity. People were beginning to wonder whether he had actually been buried at all.

At last, the local clergy decided to hold a group exorcism, with as many priests as they could muster from the surrounding parishes. Strength in numbers was their hope, but hope was soon defeated. As eleven of them congregated in Porlock church and began the service of exorcism, they were joined by a rare visitor to that place. This was Lucott himself, whose lewd and taunting behaviour appeared even more unacceptable given the setting. As the service progressed, he became more menacing, and charged down the aisle at the group which had gathered near the altar for protection. They all fled.

Spurred on by this victory, Lucott's behaviour got even worse. Another plea went out to priests far and near, in the hope that a twelfth might accomplish what eleven had not – this being the blessed number of the apostles. It was answered by the priest from St Decuman's Church, a particularly holy shrine above Watchet. (Indeed, St Decuman himself had shown little regard for the laws of nature when it came to those who should, or should not, be considered dead.)

The newcomer invited Lucott to come for a ride, and Lucott was too curious at this new tactic to refuse. A horse was quickly found for him, and he and the priest rode along the coast to Doniford, a less populated part of the shoreline. A small crowd gathered on the stony beach to see what would happen next.

The priest held something in his closed hand which he dared Lucott to eat. Lucott craned forward to see what it was – as did the spectators. The ghost lashed out at the nearest bystander with his customary viciousness, taking out the poor man's eye.

'And that's fer yer damned impiddence!' he cried.

'Oh, a brave man you are,' said the priest. 'But I dare say not brave enough to eat this.'

He opened his fingers and there, on his palm, everyone could see a holy wafer.

'You're a fool if you think that holds any terrors for me,' said the brute as he reached out to take it.

Seemingly out of nowhere, a little breeze sprang up and whisked the holy wafer away.

'You must be glad about that,' said the priest, tauntingly. 'But do not be distressed, I have another about me.'

Somehow the fitful little breeze had become a steady wind.

'Never fear, I know what to do to avoid the same mishap.'

The priest took an empty snuffbox from his pocket. Opening the lid just a sliver, he slipped the wafer inside. Lucott made an impatient move to grasp it, but the priest held it just out of reach.

'Open the box, I cannot reach the cursed thing like that!'

'Oh, but I think you can, a man of your powers …' said the priest, teasingly.

As they all watched, Lucott shrank and twisted until he seemed to be nothing more than a wisp of dark smoke that curled itself through the crack beneath the box's lid. The priest snapped it shut and flung the box far out over the waves, where it sank beneath the sea. And that is how the people were rid of Lucott's troublesome ghost … although, those locals who know this story live in fear that a strong tide, combined with a meddlesome beachcomber, may bring him back.

The natural barrier of the Severn Sea halted the progress of the Saxon invasion. On its far side, the ancient Britons, now known as the Welsh, were able to retain and develop their culture

without the constant destruction and interruption of war. Hermits and missionaries regularly crossed the channel to reintroduce the gospel teachings. These early Christians were not always well received, and needed to be able to look after themselves – preferably with weapons not of the physical world.

ST DECUMAN AND THE HOLY WELL

Decuman, a hermit from Wales, took up residence above the harbour town of Watchet on the Severn Sea. Despite the unusual manner of his arrival (sailing across those unpredictable waters using his cloak for a boat), not everyone was convinced that he was anything special. The sceptics were not won over even when they were told that his cloak had also borne his favourite cow.

Decuman settled by the well – already a holy site for pagans for countless centuries. There he lived peacefully. Whenever he needed a supplement to the spiritual powers which sustained him, he milked his cow. Other than prayer, this seems to have been his only activity.

Accounts differ as to whether he was tolerated, accepted or resented for his new-fangled Christian ways amidst those of the old religion. Fingers are pointed both at the local population and at a marauding Dane for his attempted murder. Whoever it was, the assailant removed Decuman's head with one stroke of his axe.

Not daunted, Decuman retrieved his head from where it had rolled down the steep hill, and carried it back to the well. He dipped it in the well's holy water and stuck it back where it belonged, the water acting like a kind of sacred glue.

The would-be murderer waited to see what would happen next – which was that Decuman proceeded to milk his cow. What does it take to convince an unbeliever? It was only when

Decuman had drunk a quantity of milk without leaks appearing that he made his first convert to Christianity. And with that one, others rapidly followed.

There is now a Christian church dedicated to St Decuman in the place where these events happened. In a corner of the churchyard is a curious and lively sculpture of a wild boar. Did the sculptor know that it was customary in the time of the old pagan religion to sacrifice and bury a wild boar just within the boundary of a sacred site? It stands beneath a yew tree; sentinel, purifier of burial grounds and sacred to the ancients.

Along an old lane, a downhill walk soon takes you north-west to St Decuman's Well. A lovingly and recently created garden welcomes the visitor. There, two tiny stone-encircled pools have been formed to cradle the flow from the original source. It wells up beneath its stone covering – though no movement can be discerned – and its water is as fresh and pure as ever. The three pools of holy water reflect the Trinity; set below them, a stone inscribed with a holy text is an invitation to peaceful meditation.

— A Dragon Tamed —

Catho, King of Dunster, was beset on all sides: the Bristol Channel in the North brought the marauding Irish pirates, the East was threatened by the invading Saxon hordes, and the marshes that fringed the wooded hill on which his castle was built were blighted by a dragon. Every night, the people took refuge in Dunster Castle and feared that the giant dragon would tear the stronghold apart with his great claws, or smoke them out with his fiery breath.

The dragon had crept out of the marshes when hunger had driven him towards the flocks in the fields and the game in the woods. The more he had eaten, the bigger he had become – the larger his size, the larger his hunger and the larger his helpings. And so it went on with increasing bulk and appetite keeping pace with one another. With all wild and domestic animals devoured, he had turned his attention to people, best attacked in groups to make the effort worthwhile. Catho's soldiers, dispatched to fight the pirates, suffered the worst of these depredations, with the dragon spitting out the melted lumps of their armour and weaponry like so many owl pellets.

Towards Dunster, through the marshes, rode the young Arthur Pendragon, recently declared High King. Everything seemed uncertain to him in this flat landscape, where he couldn't distinguish between land and sea and cloud, where land was not green nor water blue, and all surfaces took on the vast grey smoothness of the sky. Shown safely through the treacherous marshes by the local people, Arthur made his muddy way through neither earth nor water. He was thinking about how unsure his footing was amongst the powerful of his new kingdom, and how he wished he could tell friend from foe.

Arthur was riding to ask for Catho's help against the Saxons, unaware that Dunster's king was facing a more immediate threat. So wrapped up in his own worries was Arthur that he did not notice how quiet this landscape was. No birdsong carried on the brooding air; no animals moved in the grasses or stirred the reeds ...

On reaching the castle, Arthur soon learned the reason for the wry smile with which Catho greeted his request: 'I'll help you if you help me. My men are powerless in the face of a dragon that eats them by the dozen. They are yours to command if you rid me of the beast.'

It seemed only moments later that Arthur Pendragon, High King of Britain, came to be on his very own dragon quest. There he was, riding once more through the marshes, driven by need and bound by a promise that he couldn't possibly keep. He knew that his name alone would not be enough to save him, and he wondered whether the magic power of Excalibur, which protected him from the wounds of battle, also applied to those wounds inflicted by dragons. On and on he rode without sight of the dragon, until he was forced to stop because he had passed through the marshes and reached the shore of the Severn Sea.

There, as he looked out across the salty tide, he saw something strange floating in the water, something which looked as though a piece of the dawn had fallen into the sea. As the tide brought this shape of glowing colours closer, Arthur could see that it was made of rock – but this was even stranger because rock cannot float ... Now it was so close that Arthur could see that amongst the rock's rose and saffron tints were carvings of wings and crosses. Arthur dismounted and knelt on the shore, waiting for the tide to bring him the marvellous object. His hands traced the beauty of the carvings and hope filled him. He didn't want to leave this special stone alone on the beach to fall into the wrong hands. As he touched it he seemed possessed of a strength he had never felt before, and he pushed the stone beyond the tide line, where he hid it with armfuls of seaweed.

Soon afterwards, as he rode along the sands of what we now call Blue Anchor Bay, he saw a figure in the distance. He could see that it was an old man leaning on a staff, and for a moment he hoped that it was Merlin coming to help him. But this was a stranger, and as Arthur came closer he could see that the man was in some distress. When he saw Arthur, the old man cried, 'Have you seen my altar?'

The stranger introduced himself as Carantoc, a holy man from the country of Wales. He was a hermit who had spent most of his life praying in a cave until he had a vision. This vision had shown him the altar he must make, carved with crosses, angels' wings and doves. He had heard a voice telling him to set this altar upon the waters where, with the power of prayer, he would be able to make it float. He was then to follow it, and wherever it came to rest, there he was to build a Christian shrine.

'I was following it in my coracle when I was distracted by seeing a man on a horse and a mighty stirring in the marshes behind him, and then I lost sight of it.'

'Well, perhaps if you'll help me, I'll help you,' said Arthur, as he dismounted, impressed by Carantoc's magical powers.

Just then his horse bolted, and Arthur spun round at the sound of a huge and terrifying hiss. The sea turned to steam and Excalibur was suddenly uncomfortably warm to wear. The heat from the dragon's belly was turning the sand to glass as it made its hungry way towards them. Carantoc raised his staff.

'Stay,' he commanded, and the dragon stopped.

'Sit,' and the dragon sat.

'Now just cool off,' and the steam and smoke subsided. Carantoc tore off part of his robe and wound it around the dragon's neck for a collar.

'What kind of seaweed were you saying you had hidden my altar under?'

Taking the dragon by the collar, Carantoc followed Arthur to where the horse was waiting by the hidden altar. To prove that he was now thoroughly tame and had become a vegetarian, the dragon ate the seaweed whilst the horse nuzzled his new friend. The four journeyed to Dunster Castle, where Catho was as astonished as he was delighted to see them.

Carantoc made the most of Catho's good mood and extracted the funds to pay for his shrine, which was built just inland from the bay where the altar had come ashore. Arthur now had enough soldiers at his command to fight the Saxons, which they did with an enthusiasm that could only have been brought on by the joy of not being eaten.

Meanwhile, the dragon became a rather exotic household pet, relighting the cooking fires if the wind was in the wrong direction and providing a centrally heated footstool for Catho's elderly advisors. This went on until somebody younger realised that this was rather a waste of a perfectly good dragon, and he was put to work in the Severn Sea. There he swam up and down the coast from Minehead to St Audries Bay, masquerading as a great sea serpent, and putting the Irish pirates to flight. The pirates were too frightened of this monster to attempt to land, and Catho's soldiers were free to fight Arthur's enemies on other fronts. Else how different our island story might have been …

Along Somerset's coast, between Minehead and Blue Anchor Bay, this story is still remembered in wood and stone.

Every Beltane, May Eve, the 'Sailor's Hoss', a hobby horse unique in England, rises from behind the sea wall of Minehead

harbour. Boat-bodied and dragon-headed, it still guards Somerset's very own Arthur legend after many hundreds of years.

At low tide, along Blue Anchor Bay, pieces of rose pink and saffron-coloured alabaster are still to be found, known locally as Saint's or Carantoc's stone. Nearby Carhampton remembers him in street names and, when the vicar started building works beneath the vicarage to enlarge his wine cellar, an ancient shrine was discovered.

Today's world finds Carantoc's dragon shape-shifted into Hinkley Point nuclear power station. Its fierce inner heat is tamed for our daily use and converted to a continuing defence of these shores. Some say that it will not be tame forever, and, if this is true, who amongst us could subdue it?

— CREATURE FROM THE SWAMP —
A PREHISTORIC DISCOVERY

At Somerset's western edge, just before Exmoor surrenders itself to the Devon border and the North Devon coast, lies the beautiful seaside town of Porlock. Even further west is its cousin, the tiny village of Porlock Weir, with its diminutive harbour and minute Turkey Island reached by a footbridge. Between the two lies Porlock Marsh, which until recently drained sweet water from the hills of Exmoor into the sea, and provided grazing for cattle.

This landscape was dramatically changed during the October storms of 1996, when a ferocious sea breached the shingle wall that stretched between Porlock Weir and the hamlet of Bossington. Overnight, it was transformed into salt marsh. Furthermore, the storm waves peeled away layers and layers of silt, 40ft deep, that had been accumulating for thousands of years.

Palaeontologists flocked to the area when some enormous bones were discovered, exposed in what had been an ancient drainage channel. It was clear that they were extremely old because of where they were found. At first, however, no one knew from which animal they had come – perhaps a whale, as they were so large.

There was much excitement when they were identified as the pelvic and leg bones of an aurochs – the giant prehistoric bovine that was the ancestor of all our domestic breeds. These enormous animals, depicted in prehistoric cave paintings throughout Europe, stood 6ft high at the shoulder. Their massive bulk and huge spreading horns belied their turn of speed, powered by tightly packed hindquarters and neat hooves. The aurochs were very aggressive, and our ancestors needed both courage and skill to hunt them.

This find was particularly significant as it is one of only three in the whole of England. Forensic science revealed that the Porlock Marsh specimen was a mature male who had survived a range of injuries consistent with fighting other bulls. As he died around 1500 BCE, it is thought that he may have been one of the last survivors in Britain.

Shortly after this discovery, it was decided to celebrate the historic find as part of the Porlock Carnival. Wendy Dacre, textile artist and giant-maker, was smuggled across the Devon border and commissioned to make a life-size portable model of the beast to lead the carnival procession. She was specifically instructed to make a female aurochs – the committee perhaps fearing that a male might run amuck, or challenge any domestic bulls encountered along the carnival route to mortal combat. Others say that the decision was based on a romantic hope that the two aurochs could magically call to each other across the mists of time.

The female aurochs was duly constructed undercover, behind the Porlock Visitors' Centre in the days leading up to the carnival. All were welcome to assist, whether visiting tourists or local inhabitants, and Wendy's task was both helped and hindered by the contributions of passers-by.

In her quest for authenticity, she went to the very spot where the bones had been found, to extract the mud in which they had lain for so many hundreds of years. This bluish-grey substance was used to coat the aurochs' legs. It could certainly be said that the new aurochs had its feet firmly planted in history. Wendy nearly made history too, as the mud was so glutinous that she was almost sucked under. Fortunately, she just managed to extricate herself, sparing future palaeontologists the trouble of determining which species her bones belonged to.

On the appointed day, the magnificent aurochs was paraded around her ancestors' stomping ground. When the carnival was over, she was returned to the Visitors' Centre where she was destined to become its main exhibit. Here, however, there was an unforeseen problem – as, having been built outside the Centre, no one had anticipated that she would be too large to get through the door. Temporary quarters were therefore arranged for her in a nearby barn. Although local children thoughtfully provided buckets of water and oats, it could only have been the docility of her sex that allowed her to put up with these inferior arrangements.

In due course she managed to gain entrance to the Centre – when the local butcher hacked off her legs and she was carried in sideways. There she remains, on top of a huge cupboard, gazing wistfully down at the glass cabinet in which her famous relative's leg bones reside.

― THE FAIRIES AND THE FARMER'S CATTLE ―

It had been such a dry spring that nobody could remember another like it, and the farmwife – like everyone thereabouts –

could not keep up with the watering. The rain barrels had long been dry and the stream was barely a trickle – too low by far for watering the cattle and horses. She was hard put to keep their troughs and buckets filled. The vegetable garden had been left to its own devices and even the little rowan tree by the front door had perished.

When she came down on May morning, the farmwife instantly knew that something was wrong. The fire that she had banked up before going to bed had gone out. It had never done that before. There was also an unaccountably large pile of ash in the hearth. Not only that – when she went to milk the cows, the smallest would yield no milk and lowed pitifully.

Next day it was the same, only the pile of ashes in the hearth was bigger than ever. The largest cow seemed too weak to do anything other than lie in the straw, and when the farmwife finally got her to stand, she was so thin that you could count all the bones in her body. The farmwife also noticed that half the woodpile was gone.

Something was afoot, and she told her husband that she meant to get to the bottom of it. This would not be the first time that someone had had their cattle ill-wished by one of the neighbourhood witches, although the farmwife always took care not to offend anybody, and invited all to the harvest supper, whether they worked on the farm or not.

She decided to find out first what was making the fire go out. Her husband offered to hide in the great kitchen with his cudgel and blunderbuss at the ready, but she knew that he could never keep awake after ten o'clock, and that his snores would warn any evil-doer of his presence before they neared the front door.

'No husband, for you do need your sleep, and the farm will be worse off without that gurt strength of yorn tomorrow.'

So it was she who hid herself in one of the kitchen's ample cupboards, and watched and waited. Shortly before midnight, the door burst open and a host of the fairy folk poured into the room. It seemed as though the entire fairy court was there, complete with their king and queen.

'Let the feasting begin,' cried the Queen, and the fairies rushed off to make ready. Some returned carrying the rest of the wood-pile. Others reappeared – to the farmwife's mingled amazement and horror – with her husband's prize bull, wearing a garland of flowering hawthorn around his huge neck. She could barely believe her eyes when she saw the King of the Fairies pluck a single thorn from the garland and cut the bull's throat with it.

She watched, terrified, as the fairy host butchered the bull. They flayed the carcass meticulously, so that there were no unnecessary cuts or scratches on the hide, which they folded and laid to one side. Then they carefully scraped all the bones clean of flesh without nicking any of them. When the bones had all been gathered into a great pile, the cooking began. The beef pies, steaks, broths, stews, patties and sausages would have put any human cook to shame, and the farmwife momentarily forgot her fear as she made mental notes for future recipes. When every single scrap of beef had been eaten, the fairies set to playing games with the bones. They juggled them, jumped over them, played catch and piggy-in-the-middle, until the whole kitchen seemed to shimmer and heave like a cloud of fleas, and the farmer's wife grew quite dizzy. Then she heard the King of the Fairies call out: 'It will soon be dawn. Gather up the bones!'

One ankle-bone was in full flight as this order was given, and it landed right by the farmwife's foot, which was holding open the cupboard door so that she could peer through the gap. Just as a fairy was about to chase after it, quick as the flick of a whip she nudged it towards the back of the cupboard, lest she be discovered.

'Lay out the skin and arrange the bones!'

She watched as the fairies stretched out the bull's hide and laid each bone down in its correct place. She thought her heart would stop when a fairy cried out that a bone was missing. She prayed for her heart to stop when the fairy who had missed his catch turned with a frown towards her hiding place.

'No time, no time, the nightingale falls silent!'

The Fairy King touched the bull's hide with his wand and the beast lumbered to his feet and was led back to his stall.

Now she knew what she needed to do. In the dawn light, she replaced the dead rowan tree and planted another at the back door for good measure. She nailed sprigs of holly above every window too – and all this before her husband had stopped snoring. When she had given him his breakfast, uncooked for the first time since they were married, she told him what had happened.

'What a dream you did have m'dear. I should take a dose if I were you!'

But he had to swallow his words when he saw a whole season's worth of wood gone and no cart tracks to account for it. Although the cattle were restored to full health, there was a tear in his eye when he noticed how his prize bull limped for the rest of his days. As for the farmwife, her cooking became the envy of all her neighbours, and there was no accounting for the ways she had with beef …

Two

THE FERTILE GROUND
Fields and Orchards

Somerset is known for its extensive and unspoiled countryside; whether meadow, marsh, or hills too steep and rugged to be farmed, it is being rediscovered as one of England's forgotten rural treasures.

The government invented another county to put Bristol in and, since this act of piracy, Somerset has boasted no large towns comparable with those of England's industrial heritage. It is, however, the proud owner of one of the smallest cities in Britain: beautiful Wells, with one of the most perfectly preserved inhabited medieval streets in Europe.

Much of Somerset's rural landscape is populated by tiny settlements hidden in the wooded dimples of its hills. Since the extensive drainage works which began in the Middle Ages, the villages have followed the smooth curves of water-rounded slopes, and mushroomed along the narrow tracts of land revealed by the retreating marshes.

Amongst these are to be found the 'Thankful' or 'Blessed' villages – some of the very few and fortunate English communities not to lose any of their men in action during the First World War. Historical research continues, but as things stand today, Somerset – due to sheer luck in where her regiments were sent – has more than twice as many such villages as any other county.

Unlike her neighbour Wiltshire, with its rolling sweep of Salisbury Plain, limitless sky and huge fields and pastures, Somerset's agricultural land comes in small packages. Distant horizons are afforded only by the untameable: marshes glow copper as they swallow the sunset, the jagged summits of Mendip's gorges echo with the cries of peregrines, and the heights of Exmoor ring to the roar of the red stag.

Somerset is famous for its cider and apple orchards. Apples are the latest of the fruit trees to blossom, and, when they do in May, the countryside is covered in a scented tide. Their pink foam caresses the riverbanks and overflows onto the roadsides, and their most delicate of perfumes reach everywhere on the breeze.

Especially in spring, it is hard to believe that eighty per cent of orchards have been ploughed under, a trend which some of the more enlightened agencies are currently trying to reverse. Most of the orchards were planted with cider-producing varieties, and this hallowed beverage has experienced a rise and fall in fortunes to rival those of any courtier. Supplanting the weak beers consumed by the common folk and the mead preferred by the wealthier Saxons, it became the favoured drink of the aristocracy in Norman times.

In the 1960s, as incomes rose, imported wines became more sought after and affordable, and so cider, thus humbled, fell out of fashion. Currently, interest is being reawakened with national advertising campaigns for foreign imports from Ireland and Belgium, often flavoured with other fruits. In Somerset, these impostors stay on the shelf whilst we take our firkins round to the local cider farm to be filled with our chosen blends, mixed especially for us by those with generations of expertise behind them.

The county, host to so many apple trees, honours them at its very heart. The area around Glastonbury Tor is still referred to by its ancient name: the 'Isle of Avalon', the Island of Apples.

~ THE GOLDEN APPLE ~

King Edmund was a far-sighted man, and loved to hear stories from the distant lands that he longed to visit. Sailors knew that they would always find a warm welcome at his court if they brought a new tale or curious object from afar.

One evening at the end of summer, before the autumn storms that would bring the sailing season to a close, a seafarer brought the King something wrapped in a leather bag. Though small, it was very heavy. The King could hardly wait for his courtiers to retire, so that he could examine this novelty in privacy.

At last he was in his own chamber. There, a small fire burned brightly. Under a huge oak table an old hound was sleeping, and a beeswax candle suffused the room with its honey-laden scent. King Edmund placed the leather bag on the table, but before opening it he reached down and fondled his dog's ears. His old friend rolled over and sighed with contentment.

The King pulled a shining sphere from the bag. It was solid gold, cast and beaten into the exact likeness of a ripe apple. He marvelled at the detail – the puckering of the skin, the slant of the stalk, the curl of the single leaf clinging to it. There was even a tiny golden fly sipping at a dewdrop caught in the dimple between fruit and stem. He turned it over and over, each time noticing something new, but it was his fingertips that first found the lettering. He brought the candle nearer so that his old eyes could see what he had felt, and there, chased all around the base, were the words: 'Give me to the one you love the best.'

Well, that shouldn't be too difficult. Just then, his dog whimpered as he followed the running deer in his dream – and Edmund thought to himself: 'Loyal companion of so many years, always at my side throughout the long days, who else can I better trust? We are both in the twilight of our lives, how will I find another such as you when you have left me for the first and last time?'

The King was just about to pass the dog the golden apple when he heard the sound of hurrying footsteps – unmistakably the Queen's, who was the first woman in England to wear high heels. The dog woke with a soft growl and the door flew open as the Queen burst into the room. She pounced on the golden apple: 'So *that's* what you have been hiding from me! What a beauty!'

Before the King could protest, she had made off with it. The Queen examined it in her own chamber and her keen eye immediately found the inscription: 'Give me to the one you love the best.'

Well, that was going to be easy. That very night she had an assignation with the captain of the guard. Knowing that they were going to be busy, she slipped the apple into the pocket of his jerkin as soon as he took it off. They were indeed so busy that the captain was in danger of being late for his duties. The season was still warm and, as he grabbed his clothes, he didn't put on his jerkin. It wasn't until his watch was over that he first noticed how it was weighted to one side. He smiled at the apple's cunning workmanship, and in the clear morning light he immediately made out the inscription: 'Give me to the one you love the best.'

Well, that was *not* going to be easy. There were the first and third ladies-in-waiting, there was the French envoy's sister – if she really was his sister – and there was the visiting princess from Wales. As lovely in their own ways were the apothecary's wife, the priest's mistress and the pastry cook's cousin, and so the list went on … At last, the captain decided to give the apple to young Kate, the kitchen maid. She was too young even to have been kissed, and he meant to be the first to do so. This gift could be the chance he had been waiting for.

'Why ever do they make so purty a thing such a gurt weight? 'Tis far too grand a bauble for I, Sir,' said Kate, slipping it into her apron pocket.

Any further developments were postponed by the cook bustling in and giving young Kate a set of instructions. The captain sloped off to other pleasures, and Kate spent the rest of the afternoon fetching and carrying, washing and scrubbing. At last, the cook came to her carrying a baby, whose outraged yelling had made his cheeks even redder than Kate's. 'My great nevvy is that fractious with the teething and there's none to look after him what with his mother at Old Mother Sheppey's having a bad tooth drawn herself,' said the cook. 'His crying has got me that distracted, I've spoiled two lots of pastry and bested Old Alfred hisself with burning the tansy cakes. Do take this young varmint outside so as a body can have some peace before I starts putting vinegar where honey should rightly be.'

Kate carried the screaming infant into the orchard, delighted to leave the dark, smoky kitchen and be out in the fresh air. Ripe apples were already dropping from the trees and the grass was dotted with windfalls. The heavy scent of their fermentation rose from the ground, and some sheep were sleeping off the effects of their seasonal dose of alcohol. Others, not yet tipsy enough, were staggering to the next mouthful, and their contented chomping provided the percussion to the steady drone of the drunken wasps.

'They wopses is gone so far over as to be so harmless as turtle doves,' murmured Kate, as she flicked a wasp from one of the fruits and placed a harder piece into the baby's mouth to help with the teething. Setting the child down in the grass, she felt the lump in her apron pocket. Looking at the apple again, she noticed the writing – but, as she couldn't read, she was untroubled by its message.

The golden gleam caught the baby's eye. He stopped crying and held up his chubby hands for the toy. Peace came at last as Kate rolled it towards him. Gurgling, he rolled it back to her, delighted with his new game. Time drowsed on as they rolled the apple to and fro, when – at last – young, overworked Kate sank down upon the ground and fell asleep in the setting sun.

Amidst the munching sheep and droning wasps, the baby began to feel all alone. His little face was beginning to pucker up again, when into the orchard wandered a large, old dog. He lolloped up to the child and licked him thoroughly. The delighted infant reciprocated by rolling the apple for him. The dog retrieved it in his soft mouth and graciously returned it. The baby was keen to share his new game with an expert. To and fro rolled the golden apple, until, tired out with crying and playing, the little one fell asleep.

Just then, King Edmund strolled into the twilit orchard. This was where he loved to come if he could get away from

the cares of the court. In the lingering light, he sat down wearily on an old wooden bench. His beloved dog lumbered over to him, and dropped a golden apple into his lap …

There is a legend from the West – so ancient that only fragments remain – that when people first came to the land of Britain, they called it Honey Island.

～ As Sweet as Honey ～

Samuel was so poor that he didn't think things could get any worse. When they did, he knew that he would have to leave the only place he had ever known and go to the town to look for work. So, he went to his orchard (where he still kept some beehives) to tell the bees that he was leaving, and that he didn't know when he would be back. He took a last long look at the few remaining apple trees, remembering when the sheep, pigs and geese had roamed amongst them. Then he set off for the town, only knowing which way to go because the carter who passed by every few months had once pointed it out.

Poor Samuel did not know what a town was – he had never seen one. He only knew that many people lived there, and that those without enough to eat were called beggars. He supposed that he must be a beggar too because he had been hungry for a long time, but the carter had told him that he could find work, and that's what he meant to do.

Samuel hadn't realised how far away the town was. He had walked for two days and two nights on an empty stomach, and there seemed no end to the forest. As night fell on the third day of his journey, it was the dark of the moon and the stars were hidden by clouds. Fearing to stray from the path and lose his way, and being too faint with hunger to go much further, Samuel found a hollow amongst the roots of a huge dead tree in which to shelter for the night. It was surprisingly warm there, and his dreams were filled with strange murmurings and rustlings. When hunger woke him, it seemed that sleep had soothed away all his troubles.

Now the murmuring and rustling followed him into wakefulness, swelling to a pervasive hum. Samuel had gone to sleep in a hive of wild bees. Feeling no fear, he spoke to them as he had always done to his bees at home. As he was now a beggar, he begged them for honey, and the bees suffered him to break off a piece of honeycomb. This he ate in the sunlight, and strength and purpose returned.

'Thank you bees, I won't forget you!' he said, and he was on his way.

At last he reached the town, and looked with mingled wonder and dismay at its scurrying, heaving mass of people. They were pouring down the streets and swarming into the square in which he found himself. Their voices buzzed with an edge of anger and fear. The place reminded him of a disturbed hive. His gaze travelled up the cobbled slopes, and his mouth and eyes grew rounder with every breath as he stared at a building larger than he could ever have imagined. It was the King's castle. He had never thought that such a bewildering complexity of bridges, staircases, windows, courtyards and towers could exist. And now there were soldiers pushing through the crowd, searching. Searching for him.

'There's a stranger! I'll wager he hasn't been before the King yet. Speak up you, has the King asked you already or not?'

Samuel looked so bewildered that they decided the interview couldn't yet have happened, and so they hustled him up the cobbled streets towards the castle. He barely knew which questions to ask to find out what was happening, but managed to learn that the King had a passion for riddles – and if the latest riddle couldn't be answered, he flew into a passion of a different sort.

Today he had asked a riddle that no one could answer. Although excellent solutions had been offered, the King's fury had reached new heights, and every person in the town who could speak had been ordered to attempt to solve his riddle. Now that the King was threatening to have the next provider of the wrong answer beheaded, strangers were especially welcome.

Samuel soon found himself in the castle, being dragged through those confusing courtyards and corridors, and then he was in the presence of the King. Or so he assumed, as there was nothing regal about this man's behaviour, the crown on his head being the only clue. He was charging up and down, bellowing like a bull in a bate – and Samuel knew only one way to make him stop before he did himself an injury. He grabbed him and held him tight in his great strong arms – the way he would with any desperate animal on the farm. The shocked soldiers rushed forward, but realised that, as the two men were so close, they risked doing the King an injury if they intervened.

'Shh! Shh! Your Majesty, now don't take on so …' and Samuel put a firm finger over the King's lips before he could roar the next round of outrage.

The King relaxed immediately. He returned Samuel's embrace and kissed him on both cheeks. 'Well done my boy, well done, you've solved it!'

'Solved what, Your Majesty? How can that be? No one has yet told me what the question is!'

'Come, come, don't remind me of how many times I have had to ask it today! None of my numbskull advisors could tell me the answer to 'What is the sweetest thing in the world?' – and you have done so without a word! And as for all that sentimental claptrap about a baby's first smile, and a maiden's first kiss, what stuff and nonsense – of course, it's honey! Honey is the sweetest thing in the world, as any fool would know – except mine,' said the King, aiming a kick up the backside of his fool, who was, as usual, in the wrong place at the wrong time.

'Less common sense than a half-wit,' growled the King.

'Sire,' said the fool, 'why is common sense so rare?'

'That sounds like another riddle, Fool.'

'Yes, Sire, one to which there will never be an answer!'

The King paused for a moment, then burst into laughter.

'Very good, Fool, very good …' and with the King's restored good humour standing the test, everyone breathed a sigh of relief. So it was that Samuel's honey-sticky finger solved a riddle without him even knowing what it was, when no one else could.

'Thank you bees,' he breathed. 'I shan't forget you.'

The King bustled off arm-in-arm with Samuel and the fool, for it was suppertime, and the King's new best friend was to dine at his right hand. There were smiles all round – with one exception, which Samuel didn't notice as he was so busy eating. The King's chief advisor was jealous of this new-found favourite, and his eyes glittered with malice whilst others beamed. He could barely hide his scowl when the King announced that he was immediately appointing Samuel as another advisor.

Courtly life continued to bewilder Samuel, and he was always getting lost in the castle with its logic-defying twists and turns – but, whenever advice was needed, his common sense prevailed where others' expertise failed, and the King continued to be pleased with him.

Meanwhile, the chief advisor was plotting ways to get rid of Samuel – not a difficult task for one who was so twisted, scheming and dishonest. Whilst in the position of greatest trust, he had over the years been secretly robbing the King's treasury, cunningly ensuring that the stolen treasure never left the castle. What better place to hide it? From time to time he had given orders for the very structure of the castle to be altered: a staircase declared unsafe and leading nowhere in order to hide a secret room; a wall blocked off so that the gallery behind would be, in time, forgotten; a secret escape passage constructed for 'the King's safety' – just in case – with the workmen disappearing shortly afterwards. Now these changes were to serve him in another way ...

The chief advisor wasted no more time. Before the newcomer could establish himself further, he said to the King: 'Sire, there is more to this clever stranger than meets the eye. What do you know of him? What does anyone know of him? He pops up out of nowhere with the solution to a riddle that a whole town cannot solve, whilst declaring that he didn't even know the original question. How likely is that? Who is to say that he hadn't been here for some time and heard the question being discussed by your loyal subjects, as it must have been the talk of the town? It is never wise to be too trusting. I advise that this young man be put to the test.'

The King began to feel uneasy. He wasn't sure whether it was because his chief advisor always managed to pour cold water on his enthusiasms, or whether there was some truth in what he was hearing. The chief advisor made the most of the King's discomfiture:

'Of course, Sire, I trust that you have not forgotten the other kinds of riddles?'

'Other kinds of riddles?' said the King, looking startled. 'What do you mean?'

'Riddles of action, not just of thought, Your Majesty.'

'Riddles of action? No idea what you're talking about!'

'Like setting somebody a difficult task to do, a kind of test that demands courage and ingenuity …'

'Sounds like some kind of fairytale nonsense to me,' said the King. But he was intrigued and could not resist adding: 'Another sort of riddle do you say?'

'Quite so, Your Majesty. It could be rather fun. What if he were set a task in keeping with his new position? He is supposed to be your loyal servant, loyal to you and what this castle represents, yet he seems more fitted to finding his way about a barn or a pigsty. Why, he can barely find his way between the great hall and your own chamber! What if his task is to make a perfect model of the castle within a day?'

'That sounds rather difficult,' said the King, 'and what if he couldn't do it? What would his forfeit be?'

'I'm sure we'll think of something, Your Majesty …'

And now someone else was thinking. It was the fool, sitting under the table, picking his toes, forgotten by the King and unnoticed by the chief advisor. He could tell which way the wind was blowing, and he feared for Samuel. As soon as he could leave unseen, he ran to warn him. Samuel was frightened – he knew he could never accomplish such a task, he knew he was no match for the chief advisor's ill will, and, with nowhere else to go, he fled back to the forest.

Meanwhile, an announcement was made to the whole court that, for their entertainment and protection, the new advisor would shortly be put to the test and asked to solve a different kind of riddle. When Samuel did not appear at the appointed time to learn what it was, his persecutor was gleeful.

'You see, Sire, an impostor indeed. Surely if he ever had any extraordinary powers, he would be here to demonstrate them.'

On hurried Samuel through the forest, instinctively going in the direction of home. There was no sign of pursuit, but he couldn't tell if this was because his absence hadn't yet been discovered. At last he had to rest, and he looked for somewhere near the road where he could remain hidden in case the soldiers had been sent after him.

There was a dark hollow beneath a great dead tree. Bees darting in and out buzzed a friendly greeting, danced on his sleeves, and gently skimmed his hair and the backs of his hands. He crept into the shallow cave where their hive was.

'Oh bees, how could I have forgotten you when you helped me in my need?'

The warm, murmuring darkness accepted him once more, and once more he spoke to the bees and told them all his troubles. Every time he mentioned the chief advisor, their comforting hum turned into an angry buzz. At last, his story told, he fell into a deep sleep.

When he awoke, the first thing he saw was the queen bee herself sitting on his hand not six inches away from his face. She waved her feelers and danced on her legs, and Samuel knew she was saying something important. If only he could understand the bees the way they seemed to understand him! She made little rushing flights towards the mouth of the hollow, always returning to his hand, and he knew that he was meant to follow. Carrying her carefully into the light, he saw that the drones were waiting for him on the path, all lined up in an arrow formation. The arrow was pointing back to the castle. As he emerged, the arrow took off, flew towards the castle, wheeled back and hovered above Samuel's head, before flying forward a few feet and then returning for him. It was clear what the bees were telling him – to return to the castle.

He decided to trust them. As soon as his stride became purposeful, his humming escort left him.

If Samuel had glanced back, he would have seen what appeared to be a great cloud of swirling black smoke leaving the hollow and rising high above the trees. The cloud billowed and swelled, gathered itself and made a bee-line for the castle. If anyone there had looked up, they would have seen this miniature tornado reach the highest of the battlements – and then melt away into thin air.

The bees worked individually, each one exploring a different part of the castle. There was no crack or keyhole that they could not squeeze through in order to examine every nook and cranny of that vast building. Then, with one accord, each scout left his allotted task as they converged in the great hall. The court was out hunting, and any remaining servants had taken the opportunity to catch up on their rest. The hall was empty – save for the swarm, which filled it with its buzzing busyness as each bee danced to his companions where he had been and what he had seen.

Amongst the returning hunting party, the fool was the only one to look up. He smiled as he saw the swarm of bees flying towards the forest.

'Look, Sire, there go the bees to make more sweetness for us.'

When the court entered the hall, all marvelled at what awaited them. There, on the table, was an exquisite miniature castle, moulded from wax. It was their castle – complete in every last detail. They recognised the familiar chambers and passages. The room where they were now standing had each feature perfectly represented, down to the broken arch of one of the windows and the slant of the fireplace. It was so true to life that it seemed only to lack the animation of tiny people and animals. Some would not have been surprised to see them, and wondered whether the castle had been created by the fairy folk. But it had not been made by them ... unless fairies work in wax.

The King peered closer.

'Bless my soul! I never knew that those rooms existed – I always wondered why that staircase seemed to lead nowhere! Surely that's a passage my father never showed me – and whatever can that be, all down its length?'

Not only had each 'secret' chamber now been revealed, but also their contents: tiny treasures, each gilded with the gold of the bees' honey. As the chief advisor stared at this small miracle, for the first time in his life, his rage was tempered with fear.

Tired, dusty and footsore, Samuel reached the castle gates – and was very surprised when the guards bowed low before him. He limped into the great hall and was embraced by the King.

'Well done my boy, well done! You've done it! Done it again, and again without even knowing what the task was!'

Samuel blushed at the applause, looked round at the beaming faces – and almost staggered at the hatred on his enemy's countenance. The danger was increasing, as the well-meaning King gave orders to the guards to break down the walls to the passage and chambers, to see if they really did contain treasure. Then to his horror, Samuel heard the King say, 'And if you're right in this, my boy, maybe it's you who should be appointed my chief advisor ...'

'Oh no, Your Majesty, I'm sure that couldn't be right,' he mumbled, hanging his head in his confusion, not daring to catch the chief advisor's eye. He stared down at his feet, desperate to come up with something to break the King's train of thought, when he blurted out:

Two brothers are we, great weights we bear
Hard, hard we are pressed.

We are full in the day and the last is to say
That at night, empty we rest.

'What's that?' said the King, 'Boy's gone quite mad. All this excitement's turned his wits.'

'It's a new riddle, Sire, that I learned on my travels':

Two brothers are we, great weights we bear
Hard, hard we are pressed.
We are full in the day and the last is to say
That at night, empty we rest.

The King was thrilled to be told a new riddle. Usually it was the other way round. Quick as a wink, he said, 'Eyes, the answer is eyes!'

'Very good, Your Majesty, but wrong!'

The fool leaped onto the table and started to walk round the model of the palace on his hands. His feet waggled in the air as he licked the honey from the wax treasure. One foot found the other and nudged off a shoe. Balancing on only one hand, he caught his shoe as it fell, and flung it at the chief advisor. As the court gasped, he did the same with the other. The chief advisor unsheathed his sword at the insult and lunged. But the fool had already sprung into a tumble, so the sword missed him and the point sank into the wax throne.

There was another gasp, and the fool was on his feet, bowing to the chief advisor:

'Sir, you mistake me. I was merely giving you the answer to the riddle. Surely it is shoes!'

'Surely it is!' cried Samuel.

'Well done, Fool, well done!' cried the King, cutting a caper as the guards carried in the riches that had been missing from the treasury for years.

If there was any part of the chief advisor that had not been eaten up by rage and fear, it was now consumed by humiliation. Furthermore, he now had two enemies instead of one. It was even more urgent to get rid of Samuel before awkward questions were asked about how the treasure had been hidden.

'Majesty,' began the chief advisor loudly, when the court had assembled to dine, 'as this young man is so adept at finding treasure that no one even realised was lost, how about making use of his services to find that most precious item that went missing just before your coronation?'

'You mean my fa …'

'Quite so,' interrupted the chief advisor. 'No need to spell it out, since our new friend always seems to know what the test is, even before he is told.' He gazed threateningly at the fool as though daring him to speak, but the fool knew better. The scrutiny was maintained in case he tried to whisper to Samuel, but the fool was taking no chances, and seemed more interested in chasing a particularly annoying flea.

The constant movement as he searched for it drew all eyes to him, and there were ripples of laughter at his contortions to reach it. Then his eyes seemed to follow its movement as it leaped onto the table to escape, and the thump from the fool's slap on the tabletop made all the dishes rattle. The fool examined the palm of his hand minutely but was not satisfied. Everyone followed his jumping gaze as it seemed to follow the flea's hops in an unerring zigzag towards the chief advisor. He could stand the suspense no longer, and leaped back before a slap from the fool could be explained away as a helping hand. How they all laughed! As they did so, the fool contrived to knock over the honey pot, and the King laughed loudest with delighted disgust as the fool dipped his long sleeves in the spill and squeezed honey into his mouth from their tips.

Simmering with fury, the chief advisor looked away to regain his composure, just as Samuel watched more closely. One sleeve was now being used to dribble honey onto a piece of bread. The crust framed it like a picture. It was a picture, a picture of a golden crown, and then it was licked clean.

'Sire, how long do I have in which to find this crown for you?'

'Until tomorrow's sunset,' spat the chief advisor.

Samuel walked back through the forest on sore feet. This time he had not forgotten the bees, and wasted no time in reaching them. He arrived just as the hive was stirring, crept into the cool shade of the hollow tree and once again told them his trouble. Again they allowed him to break off a piece of honeycomb, but this time he smeared the honey on his feet, knowing that it would soon heal his sores and blisters. Then, tired out with his journey and his enemy's malevolence, he fell into a deep sleep.

As Samuel slept, the bees remembered the day long ago when the old king's hunting party had lost its way. The present king had only been a prince then, hardly more than a boy, and his chief advisor-to-be, though even younger, already had cruel ways. As they were emerging from the forest, he had flicked his whip at a small swarm of bees hanging from a branch. This had so angered them that a bee had stung him on the back of his neck. His cry of pain had startled his mount, making him shy into the King's horse and forcing him into a nearby stream. As the King's horse slipped and scrambled, the King was thrown. In the melee, no one had noticed that the King's crown was missing. His party had hurried him back to the castle where he could be cared for.

Some time passed before servants were sent back to search the spot, but even if they had gone to the right place they hadn't found the crown. Its loss was seen as a bad omen and the old king never really recovered from his fall, dying soon after.

It was past noon when Samuel woke. In each of his curled palms lay a candle fashioned from beeswax, with rush stems for wicks. His humming escort was waiting outside. He followed it through the forest, along the course of a stream, and emerged at last onto rolling hills that pasturing sheep had turned into smooth grassland. Where the tree line gave way to grazing, the stream soon dipped into a hollow where there was a jumble of rocks. There the bees led him, darting through the crevices but always returning – and Samuel knew where he was meant to go.

At last he managed to prise the rocks away from what had been the mouth of a cave. This had collapsed, but he could nevertheless feel the movement of air coming from the darkness. There must be some kind of passage with another opening. Remembering the beeswax candles, Samuel lit one with his flint and forced himself into the tunnel beyond the rock fall. Holding the candle above the wet, he crawled forward until at last the candle flame was answered by another golden glow. It was impossible to turn round. He would have to crawl backwards, and because of the candle he could only use one hand. Rather than risk crushing the crown beneath his clothes, he carried it on his head. Filthy, wet and bruised, he was led back by the bees to their hive, and from there he returned to the castle.

The court was dining when Samuel placed the crown before the King. A last ray from the setting sun turned it into flame, and the King stretched his hands towards it as though to draw its warmth. Then its fire mellowed and the King turned the golden circle in his hands.

'Well done again, my boy, well done again and again. How sorry I am that my old father could not know you, and now

I too am old. Too old to rule and with no son of my own, unless it be you.' Then the King placed the old crown on Samuel's head.

Into the golden silence came a sound so dark and angry that no one could tell what it was – until the black swarm of bees swept into the hall and covered the chief advisor. He ran howling from the room, and if he ran and howled until he reached the sea, nobody cared.

'Thank you, bees, I shan't forget you,' whispered Samuel.

The first law he made was that every man, woman and child should cultivate the flowers and trees most loved by bees. New orchards blossomed, gardens were planted, and the people's lives were filled with warmth and colour.

Eastern Somerset used to be largely covered by the impenetrable Selwood Forest, which was put to the axe as the fires that smelted iron into weapons grew ever hungrier. After this came the sheep. Able to roam in these newly created spaces, they consumed the remaining undergrowth and saplings. Grassland encroached, and where there had been forest there was now rolling pasture. Sheep were here to stay.

Since then, they have been an integral part of Somerset's landscape and livelihood. They gave many of the towns – such as Shepton Mallet, Shepton Montague and Woolavington – their names, and made this region rich with wool – and leather. It was in 1825 that James Clark, whilst working in his brother's tannery, had an idea. In the confined space, the piles of offcuts from the hides kept getting under his feet, and he thought, why not make slippers with them? Thus was born Clark's shoe factory, soon to be famous throughout the country and beyond.

Today, shops on the tourist trail sell sheepskins as luxury items. They are available either in nature's 'own' colour range, or dyed in an array of shades to rival the rainbow – as befits Glastonbury, New Age capital of this earthly vibration.

> If I were a Bristol merchant-man
> With silver to collar and silver to hem
> And fine chests of gold a sight to behold
> The thieves and the robbers would soon make me old
> But I'd rather be tending my sheep
> Yes I'd rather be tending my sheep
> My ewes and my rams and my little young lambs
> I'd rather be tending my sheep.
> A shepherd I been all the days I have seen
> When the fields they are white, when the leaves they are green
> I do meet with my foe when the cold wind do blow
> And they foxes so cunning hide down in the snow
> But I'd rather be tending my sheep
> Yes I'd rather be tending my sheep
> My ewes and my rams and my little young lambs
> I'd rather be tending my sheep.

~ CLEVER BETTY ~

There was once a poor shepherd whose only daughter was as beautiful as she was bright, and as bright as she was brave. Betty's mother had died when she was a baby, which meant that the girl had learned to fend for herself from an early age. She worked here and there, wherever she could, and no one could have found fault with anything she did. As she reached womanhood, it was hard to tell whether her beauty surpassed her skill or her skill surpassed her wit.

Most days, Betty worked for Farmer Ted, a wealthy widower who was also their landlord. This farmer was as old as he was ugly, and as mean as he was rich. No one had a good word to say about him; and his name, manners and appearance begged the local wags to call him 'Farmer Toad' behind his back.

Every meal he ate, and every piece of clean linen he wore, came from Betty's hands, but the wages he put into them were little enough. However, work was scarce, and so day after day she cleaned and cooked and mended. As she worked she would fill the old farmhouse with song, and the scent of lavender followed her as she danced about her tasks. Her presence seemed to light up the darkest corners of the gloomy old farmhouse.

One day, when Betty had turned sixteen and the farmer was eating a particularly savoury lamb stew, a thought came to him – which was a rare occurrence. He realised that if Betty were his wife, he would have her hardworking loveliness about him all the time, and would never have to pay her a penny. As she served him a third helping, he grabbed her wrist and proposed marriage. Betty shook him off and, for the first time, he saw her beautiful face twist with anger: 'Never think of it; I wouldn't marry you for all the cheese in Cheddar!' she cried.

This puzzled the farmer for a few moments, until he remembered that girls like to show a false modesty for propriety's sake, acting all coy and shy, and playing hard to get. The farmer allowed a few days to elapse for the sake of her modesty and then tried again: 'Betty m'dear …'

But she flung at him: 'I told you never to think of it; I wouldn't marry you for all the boats in Bristol!'

This puzzled the farmer further and he was quite at a loss. What did it matter if he was old enough to be her grandfather? He was rich! What did it matter if he was uglier than a toad? He was rich! What did it matter if he had the manners of a boar at the trough? He was rich! He put her skittishness down to youth – not a bad thing in itself because her beauty would last longer, as would her strength for work. He resolved to speak to her father, to get him to bring his parental authority to bear.

Betty saw the old man lumbering along to their cottage on the far side of the orchard, and she knew what he was about. When she returned home, her father said, 'Betty m'dear …'

'Never think of it; I told that old toad I wouldn't marry him for all the wool in Wiveliscombe, so don't you start!'

And, for the first time in ten years, the shepherd had to get his own supper. But now he was a worried man, caught on the one side by his daughter's wrath and on the other by the demands of a master who was also his landlord. He soon received a summons to go to the farmhouse, and he was all in a sweat. When Betty saw where he was going, she knew what he was about.

Shepherd and farmer faced each other in the gloom – farmer becoming more baleful as he realised he was still to be thwarted, and shepherd fearful of losing both job and home.

'It's for the child to obey the parent; you must bring her round, and there's the end on it, or else …'

The shepherd did not know what to reply, until desperation suddenly gave him an idea.

'Sir, you knows how womenfolk don't like to make a spectacle of theirselves in company, unless it be for the showing off of a new frock and suchlike. Well this be my plan: on the eve of the Sabbath, when Betty has finished her work, you go ahead and make ready for the wedding to take place here at the farm. That way all the preparations can be kept so dark as a bat's elbow. Swear guests and witnesses to keep secret and ask them to come over after Sunday service. Priest can toddle along with all to conduct the ceremony, and he'll be so happy as a pig in straw not to have to get out of bed special for it. Have some womenfolk ready that you can trust to do 'zactly what they be told …'

'There's no woman on God's Earth will do 'zactly what she's told. T'would be a miracle of Nature and the Devil laid so low that Priest might burn his hassock!' interrupted Farmer Ted.

This combination of scientific truth and the prospect of Mother Church's imminent demise gave the shepherd pause for thought.

'Then they must be paid to obey,' he replied, emboldened by desperate circumstances. 'Do they meet Betty at the backdoor and take her upstairs where her new frock and bonnet will be ready for her …'

'You mean I will have to provide new clothes along of all the vittles and cider!' exclaimed the horrified miser, wondering whether paying for bribes and a new trousseau were quite the economies he was hoping for.

'Yes Sir, shawl and shoes and ribbons too, I shouldn't wonder, or the plan is so dead as a stillborn lamb. We don't know what women wouldn't do for new clothes – some have been known to get married for that one and only reason. When the women have taken her upstairs and dressed her in all this finery, sworn to secrecy, with never a word passing their lips …'

'Never a word passing women's lips! Two miracles of nature in one day! The Bishop of Wells will be turning the old farm into a shrine, once he do get to hear of it!'

'When they have dressed her in all this finery,' continued the shepherd, ignoring any possible future sanctifications, 'they must burn all her old clothes she arrived in. Once she's all dressed up, she's to be took downstairs where all will be waiting for the ceremony to start. She'll be that mazed before the throng, she'll not want to show herself up by being awkward, so she'll go along with it all, so docile as a rabbit avore a weasel. And if she do think twice, she won't be in a state to give the new clothes back, even if she had a mind to, which she won't on account of her being female.'

His shepherd drew breath and Farmer Ted conceded that this was the best – and only – plan of action so far. It only remained for them to figure out how to get Betty into the right place at the right time. It was at last decided that a visitor whom Betty didn't know would be sent from the farm to fetch her, 'As she be so skittish as a filly on corn, and won't be biddable by me,' said her father.

Having agreed that Betty would be more likely to follow a stranger than her own father, it only remained for Farmer Ted to bribe the congregation and make preparations for the wedding.

The shepherd returned home to a quiet and thoughtful daughter. The next day was Saturday and Betty had even more difficulty than usual extracting her week's wages from the farmer. The following morning in church, she knew something was afoot from all the whispers and sidelong glances, and no one able to meet her eyes. At the end of the service, nobody spoke to her. Betty saw them all heading off in the same direction whilst she silently returned home with her father.

There she busied herself dosing a sick old ewe, and then she led the sheep to the orchard where she could keep an eye on her whilst gathering windfalls. From beneath the apple trees, she saw a strange girl hurry to the cottage and speak to her father. Had she been close enough, she would have heard the girl say, 'I be come to fetch Betty!'

Betty could see her father pointing towards the orchard before hurrying back inside. Even from that distance, his movements looked furtive. Soon the girl was running towards her.

'I be sent to bring Betty to the farm,' gasped the girl.

'Betty be over there,' said Betty, pointing to the old sheep.

The girl looked confused for a moment. 'But I was told to fetch Betty …'

'Didn't you think to bring some rope with you? I'd best help you catch her then,' said Betty, which she did, and watched the girl drag the smelly old ewe back to the farm as she had been told – or so she thought.

As the other women had been paid to obey their instructions and not question them, it fell to the poor newcomer to query the wisdom of what was about to happen.

'Sir, Sir, are you sure we're doing right to take Betty upstairs?'

'Do you have her here?'

'Yes Sir, like you said, but …'

'Then do as you were told! Take her upstairs and see to all the rest of it, or it will be the worse for you!'

Getting the old ewe up the stairs was not an easy job, as, having been reared on the Somerset Levels, she was unaccustomed to heights. Considerable adjustments were necessary before she could be said to be wearing her wedding dress. Never had there been such an unhappy marriage of wool and silk. The bonnet and veil certainly improved her appearance, but then there seemed to be an insurmountable problem.

'Sir, Sir, there be only two shoes!'

'Of course there be only two shoes; am I expected to provide more avore she's even wore those out? The wastrel!'

The dilemma was solved by forcing one shoe on a front hoof and one behind. Unsurprisingly, the descent was no easier than the climb, but the musicians played ever louder to mask the fracas on the stairs. At last the bride was led into the throng, to the congregation's howls of laughter. The priest was by now so drunk that, much to their added entertainment, he went through most of the ceremony before noticing that something was amiss.

While all this hullabaloo was going on, Farmer Ted managed to creep away.

He left the village, and the district, seeking to hide himself in some distant part of the country where the sorry tale of his humiliation would not be heard.

Meanwhile, the old ewe was returned to the orchard – somewhat better for her dose, and none the worse for having been thrust into society. Betty moved into the farm, as she didn't think it right to leave it empty: 'On account of all they people a body couldn't trust,' she said meaningfully to her father. 'Up to their mischief when your back is turned, so dishonest as a thieving jackdaw.'

She continued to care for the place as well as ever, and paid for her wages with the occasional sale of the farmer's family heirlooms. And now that Farmer Ted was no longer there, what was it to anyone if there was sometimes a young man about the place to do what had never been women's work?

In the meantime, the story of the marriage service had spread far and wide, and had even been reported in the Bristol broadsheets. There had also been an inquiry originating from the Bishop's Palace, and the priest had been sent to pastures new. It was a long time before Farmer Ted thought of returning home, but at last – hoping that the fuss had died down – he plucked up the courage.

Creeping along the hedgerows, his heart beat a little stronger at the sight of each familiar landmark. Now that the daylight was fading, he was brave enough to enter the village. As he was passing the pub, he smiled to hear the villagers' voices lifted in song – until, that is, he came close enough to make out the words:

Oh hear the tale of Sheep and Toad
What a curious pair to be betrothed

Oh hear the tale of Toad and Sheep
We'll go to the wedding and laugh till we weep!
So long as she'll have him, warts and all
We'll all be there to dance at the ball
So long as she's there for the wedding feast
When it comes to the bedding he won't be fleeced.
So quicken and hasten, no cause for to tarry
Send for the priest, there's a sheep for to marry
The loveliest bride will be no surprise
When she's pulled the wool right over his eyes.

Farmer Ted lost no time in turning round and heading straight back the way he had come – and Betty stayed right there on the farm.

There are many recorded instances of inappropriate or unusual marriages, and the days are not so distant when having an illegitimate child was treated as an unforgivable crime. This was as much to do with financial as with moral reasons, as the maintenance for illegitimate children became a responsibility of the parish. Whatever the circumstances of the baby's conception, it was always considered better for the mother to marry, and this is how that ceremony was brought about in the case of young master Bacon …

‒ SAVING BABY BACON ‒

William Bacon, born in 1725, was blessed with rude good health. At Bridgwater Fair, at the age of fifteen, he was hired by a farmer from Stogumber. Whatever the duties of his new position, they did not require him to make love to Mary, who also worked on the farm. This romance did not last – William dumped Mary after a very brief encounter, but not before Mary had become pregnant. As her pregnancy progressed, every effort to persuade William to marry her was resisted. He absolutely refused to do so.

The authorities were determined to prevail, as they didn't want the parish to be responsible for the baby's upkeep; they forbade the farmer to give William the sack, in case he disappeared. They asked the vicar to call the banns for the marriage, but he was reluctant to do so as William's hard-hearted attitude was well known, and he couldn't see how the marriage would ever take place. But the authorities insisted that the vicar call the banns – so there would be no reason why the unhappy youngsters could not marry, when there was every reason why they should.

The village elders then set about their plan, which relied on the fact that Stogumber boasted more than one pub. They split into two groups, one team taking the vicar to one of the hostelries and the other group taking William to the second. Although the young man knew that this would turn out to be yet another ploy to get him to marry Mary (hints of financial gain had been made), he was agreeable thus far, especially as he would at least get a few free drinks if he went along.

The few free drinks turned out to be more than a few, but what neither the vicar nor the recalcitrant youth realised was that they had been spiked with untreated smugglers' brandy.

This spirit was colourless, and it was usually mixed with burnt sugar to give it the warm caramel colour that connoisseurs loved. The vapours, however, were so strong that they could make eyes stream and curl the leaves on nearby trees. There were times, after a particularly successful run, when whole villages would smell like a distillery. The fumes wafting across the fields caused rabbits to stagger and birds to fly limply around in circles. The smell could have alerted the excise men, and so on spirit-blending days all the village women would – with one accord – decide to change the filling in their quilts and burn the old goose feathers.

Before long, the vicar and the bridegroom-to-be were each so drunk that they were both incapable – incapable of saying 'No'. The following morning, still unable to stand, they were carried to the church and propped up for the ceremony by well-wishers. Fortunately, as the vicar had performed this service many times before, he was able to do so on automatic pilot. Every time William was required to give an affirmative reply, one of his minders whispered in his ear: 'Want another drink?'

William's reply was always, 'Yesh.'

He woke up in bed with Mary two days later, unable to understand why or how. When he was told that he was now a married man, he insisted on seeing the vicar.

'But I can't remember anything vicar!'

The vicar, who had always been an honest man, replied, 'Neither can I!'

But there in the parish records were the signatures, witnesses and all to prove it, and there to this day they remain.

The unkind reader may accuse other counties of stealing this story and claiming it as their own, as it may also be found in Devon and East Anglia. Rather, think of the fairy folk as having no regard for boundaries drawn on a map, and not always for those invisible borders between Fairyland and ours.

‐ The Fairy's Midwife ‐

There was once a midwife who was trusted by every woman near and far. On this particular evening she went to bed early, as although she could never count on having an undisturbed night, the following day was market-day, which she rarely missed. Of all the people in the village, she perhaps least needed the market, as grateful families were always giving her gifts of food and goods, as well as her usual fees. But she loved to go to market to see all the babies she had delivered, most of whom were now grown up, with children and even grandchildren of their own.

As could be expected, she was woken in the middle of the night by a loud knocking on her door. Outside was a rider mounted on a huge black horse. She couldn't see his face as it was deep inside the hood of his dark cloak. She didn't recognise his voice, either, when he promised her a bag of gold for her services if she came at once and asked no questions.

'I'll get my bag,' she instantly replied.

'Then take this,' he said. Reaching down, he placed a bag in her hand, which, though small, was so heavy it could only contain gold.

He swung her up behind him on the huge horse and they were off. They rode so far and so fast that she quite lost her bearings. When they finally reached their destination, she was so shaken about that the breath had been quite knocked out of her. But there was no time to delay – she was being bundled off the horse and hurried towards the most miserable, ramshackle dwelling she had ever seen. Before she had reached the door, she could hear shrill screams and squeals, like young pigs at swill time.

Then they were inside and she could see what was making all that noise, or rather who – because that large, shabby room was full of more children than she could count. Nobody would *ever* have been able to count them, as they never stayed still for long enough. They were bouncing off the few sticks of worm-eaten furniture they hadn't already broken, and, when they couldn't dislodge another sibling, they were bouncing off the walls – as were their high-pitched shrieks of delight. Her head ringing, the midwife wrenched a table leg from one of them and banged it on the floor.

'Now you all stop that noise and pandemonium, you little imps, you! Your poor mother wants some peace and quiet in her condition!'

It could have been a hundred eyes that turned their glitter towards her, as they all fell silent and stared. She stared back and it was like looking at a flock of starlings, there were so many heads that looked all alike: narrow faces, squinty eyes and pointy ears. It wasn't hard to see where their peculiar features came from, as her employer seized her arm and began to drag her upstairs. At that touch it was as though the spell were broken, and the children started bouncing and shrieking just as before.

Upstairs, a woman lay moaning on a filthy, broken bed, barely covered by a stained scrap of blanket. The bed had a leg missing and was propped precariously on a stone. Greasy ashes showed that it had been some time since the tiny grate had seen a fire. The only light came from candle stumps stuck on the head of the bed.

The midwife could tell that she would have to be quick to save mother and baby in this difficult labour. Such was her skill, that in no time she was holding the slippery, wrinkled little scrap and looking into the same squinty, glittery eyes as those in the room below. This little fellow was wasting no time in contributing to the chorus of screams and thrashing about as best as he could. He even managed to give his deliverer a punch in the eye.

'Give my little darling something to help him settle,' said the mother, with a weak smile. 'There's a flask in the chimney, bring it to me.'

As everything had already been so strange, the midwife did not question this. She reached up into the chimney and, amongst the soot and the cobwebs, her groping hand found the bottle on a ledge.

'Put some drops in my baby's eyes, that's what he needs,' said his mother, now too tired to hold him; and then she was asleep.

The midwife managed to catch his little squirming body before he wriggled off the bed, and then she unstoppered the bottle. The strangest, sweetest scent filled the room – as though all the days of summer had been gathered within. She sprinkled three drops on his eyes, and suddenly it seemed as though she was holding a cherub. He gurgled, smiled and fell asleep.

The midwife wondered what could be in that bottle. Never, in all her long years of experience amongst rich and poor, had she come across any medicine that could have such an instant, calming effect. Her eye was still stinging at the baby's unlucky blow. As she replaced the stopper, she felt some of the liquid on her fingertips and rubbed her smarting eye to see if it would soothe it.

She blinked, gasped and blinked again. Now she had a different reason to rub her eyes: that filthy room was suddenly the most beautiful she had ever been in. The furnishings were the costliest; the dirty scrap of blanket was now a coverlet of silver silk embroidered with seed pearls; the baby's wrapping no longer a moth-eaten rabbit skin, but a garment trimmed with swans' down.

'Your work here is done,' said the baby's father.

So amazed was the midwife, that she hadn't noticed him entering.

'I will take you back to your village.'

She followed him down a gracious marble staircase, its sweep leading her into a ballroom that dazzled with its many mirrors and chandeliers. It was full of the sound of the most exquisite music and thronging with a host of elegant young people. Some played instruments; some sang in haunting harmonies, whilst the rest danced gracefully together. How she longed to watch this marvellous company, but her employer was hurrying her away as quickly as he had brought her, and she found herself outside.

She shrank back against him for a moment, as she saw that their mount was breathing flames whilst his eyes glowed ruby red.

'Do not tire yet, old woman; on this steed you will soon be home.'

And so she was, as shaken and breathless as before.

It was now dawn, and hardly worth going to bed before the market. The midwife sat in her chair, between waking and dozing, and when it was time to leave for the marketplace, she could barely decide whether the night's adventures had all been a dream. There was, however, the bag of gold to convince her.

She passed slowly through the crowded square – there were so many people to greet or to ask after. Suddenly, to her great surprise, she saw the stranger from the previous night. What would he be doing at a common market? But it must be he, with his squinty eyes and pointed ears. When he turned his glittering gaze in her direction, he seemed to look straight through her with no warmth of acknowledgement or recognition. Then she saw him going from stall to stall, helping himself to goods without paying. His actions were too practised to be absent-mindedness, but nobody else seemed to notice. When he turned away, she grabbed his arm.

'Do you mean to make off with no payment?'

'Payment for what, old woman?'

'For all those things in your pockets!'

His gaze became even harder than before. 'Tell me, which eye do you see me with?'

Too startled at the question to do anything other than try to answer it, she covered one of her eyes. He disappeared. She tried covering the other – and she could see him again.

'It must be this one,' she said.

For just a moment she saw him with his cloak thrown back, a shining figure dressed in brilliant green, his pointed cap or crown so bright she could barely look at it. She saw him reach towards her, and felt fire and ice in her fairy-sighted eye as he jabbed his finger into it. Then through that eye she saw only darkness.

When she returned home, she could see with her good eye that the little bag she had been given was still there, but now it was light to the touch. Instead of the chink of gold coins came a dry rustling, and, when she opened it, she found only withered brown leaves. And for the rest of her days she saw nothing at all through the eye that had once beheld the glory of fairy glamour.

– The Brave Midwife –

Truth sometimes mimics fiction in strange and cruel ways, as in this instance of a midwife who was summoned from her cosy hearth one wild night by a loud banging at the door. She automatically fetched her bag before she went to answer it, and outside she found a darkly cloaked and hooded man on a darker horse; hard it was to distinguish them from the blackness of the night.

The man's face couldn't be seen, but his voice was clear enough when he promised her a bag of gold if she made haste to come with him and didn't ask any questions. The midwife was used to acting quickly; in her profession, minutes could mean life or death. She was lifted up behind him and they set off at a fierce pace.

There was no moon, and she had to press tightly against the stranger to keep her seat. His cloak swirled about her and she could see nothing of the way ahead. The ride was so rough and lasted for so long that she lost all sense of direction, knowing only that this was further than she had ever travelled. It seemed so far that she began to fear for the poor woman in labour. She also had plenty of time to consider her own position, and became increasingly concerned at the apparently suspicious circumstances. Why not find a midwife closer to home? Why was the fee so over-generous? Why was she to ask no questions?

She had no way of knowing that she was now in the power of Wild Darrell, a most notorious criminal who would stop at nothing to perpetrate his villainy. No one knew how this evil man managed to lead such a charmed life, as time and again he evaded all legal retribution despite his ever-increasing list of crimes.

At last they reached their destination and she was bundled upstairs to a room in which a bright fire was burning in a large grate.

The state of the mother soon made her forget her own exhaustion, as she was only just in time to save her and the baby. Needing all her skill, learned from many years' experience in using the tools of her trade, she made an incision with her serrated knife so that the tear would knit well and heal faster. Then she used the sheep-bone forceps to safely deliver the baby, who by now was blue with a weak heartbeat.

It seemed that she had only just got him breathing, and the mother clean and more settled, before the hooded and cloaked man was back in the room and hustling her out. The midwife was confused – surely now was not the time to leave the frail pair. She would have gladly sat with them through the rest of the night, or until a suitable nurse could be found. But the man brushed aside her suggestion and ordered her to make her way downstairs, where a servant was waiting with her fee and a fresh horse to take her home. He bundled her roughly out of the room and closed the door.

She stood at the top of the stairs feeling bewildered, and then realised that, in their haste, her bag had been left behind. When she turned back to retrieve it, she heard the baby give a thin cry. It was as well for the midwife that the man was facing away from the door as she opened it, and that his thick cloak stopped him feeling the draught. As she slipped in and picked up her bag, she saw him holding the child down in the fire with a poker, whilst the flames blackened his little body.

Fear and horror helped her glide swiftly and silently from the room. As soon as she was outside, a calm fury at what she had witnessed took over. She reached into her bag and took out her knife. Seizing the heavy curtain that covered the window on the landing, she swiftly and silently cut a piece of its cloth. Rearranging the curtain so that the hole could not be seen, she put knife and cloth in her pocket. Then she ran quickly down the staircase before any delay could arouse suspicion, her lips moving silently as she counted each stair.

The servant swung her up behind him on the new horse, and this journey too was made in darkness. Dawn was lightening the sky just as they passed a familiar landmark – so at least she knew from which direction she had returned. When they reached her village, she was speedily set down and a small bag of gold was flung at her feet.

That same day, she went to the authorities with her story. If inclined not to take such a fanciful tale seriously, they had to think again when she showed them the gold and the piece of cloth. And they were forced to take action when she told them to search for a big house in such and such a direction, with a precise number of stairs leading to a landing – where they would find a window-curtain with a concealed hole exactly the size of the cut piece.

Before long, the house was found and Wild Darrell was put on trial. Everyone thought that this time, finally, he would hang – but they reckoned without the brazen corruption of the judge.

Sir John Popham was well known, as he was the Lord Chief Justice and had formerly been Speaker of the House of Commons. He was also disliked – particularly in the West Country – as he had tried Guy Fawkes and Raleigh. It was unbelievable, but under his direction Darrell was acquitted. And it came as no surprise when, at Darrell's death, Popham inherited the Littlecote estates, including the lovely Littlecote Manor – the very house believed to be where this terrible murder had been committed.

The judge's wife had prayed throughout their marriage for a moderation in his behaviour, and for his soul. It is said that, in later life, she did have some influence in getting him to mend his ways – but not soon enough to avert an untimely death …

Judge Popham was hunting in a deserted spot near Wilscombe Bottom. Choosing the moment carefully, his horse threw him into the 'bottomless' pit which was to be found there. This pool was so deep that people said it led straight to Hell – and that was where Popham belonged.

Maybe, however, his wife's prayers had unforeseen results, which belong to a later story …

~ UNLUCKY JACK FINDS HIS LUCK ~

An old widow woman lived not quite alone in a tumbledown cottage. When I say not quite alone, I mean that she might have been better off if she had been. With her lived her blundering lump of a son, Jack, who was as stupid as he was lazy, and as lazy as he was stupid. All he was good for was gazing out of the window in summer and gazing into the fire in winter. In spring he stared at the floor and in autumn he stared at the ceiling. Neighbours optimistically described him as ''ooden n'eet be 'zac'ly ', or 'not exactly all there yet'.

The poverty of their miserable home increased and Jack's mother was in despair about how they were going to survive. If only she could make Jack leave home and seek his fortune! The previous summer, she had at last come up with a ruse to get Jack out of the house – by borrowing some hedgehogs from a gypsy neighbour before they were cooked, and rubbing their fleas all over Jack's chair. Unable to stand their bites any longer, Jack had rushed outside – only to haul over a block of wood, sit on it, and gaze through the window from the other side.

Months had passed. The fleas had died off in the winter and Jack had taken up his usual quarters. As it was now February, his gaze would sometimes drift from the fire to the floor. The day was turning dimpsy when the village children came singing up the lane:

Shrove Tuesday Shrove Tuesday when Jack went to plough
His mother made pancakes and she didn't know how
She boiled them she spoiled them and when they turned black
She put in so much pepper she poisoned poor Jack.
Jack's mother made pudding 'twas done in an hour
She hadn't any eggs and she hadn't any flour

She hadn't any milk and she hadn't any fat
She slapped it on the table and she said 'Jack eat that'

Rather than being offended, Mother was inspired. That night, for his supper, Jack was served nettle soup with no added water. Whilst he slept, his mother carefully removed the nails from his boots. His breakfast was genuine leather porridge, with no goodness taken out. For lunch there was hobnail pie with no added pastry. Later, Jack threatened to leave home and Mother begged him to stay – whilst serving organic toad-on-toast for his supper. Over a breakfast of scrambled free-range fleas' eggs, Jack announced his imminent departure, and no, Mother could not persuade him to stay, as she scraped the chimney for a soot stew lunch, original recipe.

'Well, what do you want to eat?' she asked with mock irritation, hopeful that her plan was working.

'Sheep's head and tripe,' came the reply.

'Then you must go into the world and search for it,' she said, tipping ladlefuls of soot into her saucepan.

So Jack left, calling out wistfully, 'Sheep's head and tripe, sheep's head and tripe …'

How far he had wandered into the world no one knew, when he fell over a bramble root. By the time he had worked out what had happened and picked himself up, he had forgotten what he was searching for. With immense effort, he managed to remember it had something to do with offal, and he renewed his travels, calling out, 'Liver and lights and gall and all! Liver and lights and gall and all!'

As he was crying out this wish list, he came across a man who had taken too much to drink and was being violently sick in a ditch. The man took exception to this apt description, smacked Jack around the head and told him rather to say: 'Pray God send no more up.'

Jack continued on his way, saying what he had been told: 'Pray God send no more up! Pray God send no more up!'

This continued until he passed a farmer sowing seeds. The farmer thought that Jack was cursing his work, smacked him round the head and made him change his message to: 'Pray God send plenty more.'

The bewildered Jack continued his journey, which chanced to pass a graveyard where a funeral was in progress.

'Pray God send plenty more! Pray God send plenty more!' heard the outraged mourners, and the enraged vicar smacked Jack round the head and told him to say: 'Pray God send the soul to Heaven.'

This he did, certain that these good words could offend no one.

'Pray God send the soul to Heaven! Pray God send the soul to Heaven!' Jack called, just as he came upon a cruel master who was about to hang his half-starved dogs. Guilt lent strength to his hand as the man smacked Jack round the head, thus giving the dogs a chance to run off. The cruel man reminded Jack that they were only animals and told him that instead he should be saying: 'A dog and a bitch about to be hanged.'

Jack's long road continued, with hunger lending a note of desperation to his cry: 'A dog and a bitch about to be hanged! A dog and a bitch about to be hanged!'

This was clearly heard by a marriage party in another church, at the exact moment in the service when all men are expected to hold their peace. The groom saw no just cause why he shouldn't smack Jack round the head, and the best man saw no impediment to helping. The kindlier bride told Jack that, instead, he should be saying: 'I wish you much joy.'

Now faint with hunger, Jack nevertheless managed to call out, as he went on his way: 'I wish you much joy! I wish you much joy!'

His path led him past a ditch in which two labourers had fallen, when the bank on which they had been working had given way. Although injured, this did not prevent one of them from leaping out to smack Jack round the head and tell him to shout: 'This one is out, I wish the other was.'

Off went Jack, by now so hungry that he yearned for the toad-on-toast he had previously spurned.

'This one is out, I wish the other was! This one is out, I wish the other was!'

Wouldn't you know it, but Jack was shouting this as he passed a one-eyed war veteran wearing an eye patch. This did not prevent the old soldier from smacking Jack round the head and exhorting him to bawl instead: 'The one side gives good light, I wish the other did.'

Jack didn't have far to go, bawling out all the while: 'The one side gives good light, I wish the other did!' before he came upon yet another church, only this time half of it was on fire. The crowd trying to extinguish the flames could hardly believe that the arsonist would draw such attention to himself. Furious people grabbed anything that came to hand to use as weapons, and then set upon Jack. The shock of having so many against him jogged his memory into remembering what it was he had come out for.

'Sheep's head and tripe is all I wish! Sheep's head and tripe is all I wish!'

The incensed mob chased him up the lane, believing he had tried to use their church as a cooking range. For all those years that Jack had never stirred himself, his legs now made up for lost time. He outdistanced his pursuers and ran all the way home. There was his mother, with the cruel man's old dog and his mate keeping her company.

Because this was the first day she could remember without Jack being under her feet all the time, she mellowed enough to make him some proper soup – but was careful to put too much salt in it.

'This isn't going to be the end of the story,' she muttered, determined not to give up her newly relished freedom quite so soon.

The next day, Jack woke up with a terrible thirst – only to be told that the well had run dry.

'What would you fancy most to drink?' asked his mother sweetly.

'A jug of buttermilk,' said Jack.

'Then you must go out into the world to work for it,' replied his mother, adding a generous handful of salt to his morning porridge.

So Jack left home again to look for work, his mother having taken the precaution of pointing him in the opposite direction from yesterday's journey.

Seeing his immense size, a farmer agreed to employ him for a day, but he soon realised how useless Jack was and asked him what he had done before. Jack regaled him with an account of the previous day's adventures – and the farmer laughed so much that he gave Jack a silver coin and sent him home.

Jack had never seen one of these before and wasn't sure what to do with it. He liked the way it sparkled in the sun, and tossed it from palm to palm. This went on until, throwing it higher into the air, he forgot to catch it on the way down and lost it. When he reached home, he told his mother what had happened.

'You gurt vool, Jack. Why ever didn't you think to stow it in your pocket?'

The next day, Jack was given work with a cowman. When it was soon obvious how useless Jack was, the cowman asked him what he had done before, and was told Jack's adventures. He laughed so much that he rewarded Jack with a jug of milk.

Remembering what his mother had told him, he squeezed it into his pocket. The milk slopped, the pocket tore, the jug fell to the ground and smashed, and he reached home in the heat of the day smelling sour.

'You gurt vool, Jack. Why ever didn't you think to place it on your head?' said his mother.

The next day another farmer hired him, and soon heard the tale of Jack's adventures. This farmer laughed so much that he sent Jack home with a round of cheese for his pains. Remembering his mother's words, Jack stumbled home trying to balance it on his head whilst being mobbed by hungry crows. What the crows didn't get, his hair did – and he arrived home with his head in a greasy tangle.

'You gurt vool, Jack. Why ever didn't you think to hold it in your hands?' said his mother.

The next day, Jack found work with a corn merchant whose store had recently been delivered from a plague of rats. He soon found out how useless Jack was and so heard the story of Jack's adventures. When he had recovered from his mirth, he rewarded Jack by giving him his best mouser. Jack remembered what his mother had told him and left carrying a huge, spitting, biting and scratching tomcat. The cat soon bit, swore and scratched his escape, leaving Jack thankful to return home empty-handed.

'You gurt vool, Jack. Why ever didn't you think to tie some string around it and pull it along behind you?'

The next day Jack was hired by a butcher, but not for long. When the butcher heard Jack's adventures, he laughed so much that he sent him home with the present of a leg of lamb. Ever faithful to his mother's words, Jack tied the leg of lamb with a piece of string and dragged it in the dust behind him. Progress was slow. He had used the only string he owned – which moments before had been holding up his trousers.

Furthermore, all the stray dogs in town were pulling at the meat in one direction, whilst he pulled in the other. It was a very sorry-looking bone that he eventually brought home.

'Barely enough for soup,' muttered his mother as she checked the salt barrel. 'You gurt vool, Jack. Why ever didn't you think to carry it on your shoulder?'

The next day, Jack worked briefly for a carter. On seeing how useless he was, the carter asked Jack what he had done before and was told his adventures. Even the old donkey in its paddock laughed at the tale, and the carter gave him to Jack as a token of their appreciation. Ever heedful of his mother, Jack lifted the donkey onto his shoulders and set off.

It was as well that he was so big and strong, but even so it was an effort and soon he was blinded by his own sweat. This led him to take a different route, and he chanced by a large manor house set in its own grounds.

Leaning out of one of the windows was the loveliest young woman – one whom Jack was in no position to notice. This young lady was an only child and had been mute from birth. Her doting father had paid doctors from far and near to cure her, but to no avail. He therefore declared that any man who could get her to utter a sound could marry her if she would have him.

Mary had never seen anything as ridiculous as a man carrying a donkey, and she started to laugh. Her father rushed over in amazement to see where the laughter was coming from, and rejoiced that his daughter had made a sound at last.

Too exhausted to continue, Jack finally put the donkey down. He was then surprised to find himself being embraced by a wealthy lord, whilst the most beautiful girl he had ever seen was covering his donkey's nose with kisses. Jack didn't know whether to be jealous of the girl or the donkey – but soon made up his mind when, to the joy of Mary's father, embraces and kisses were exchanged elsewhere and the young people agreed to marry.

Jack's mother moved in with the happy couple, and cooked him sheep's head and tripe for the wedding breakfast. Laughter was the only sound that Mary ever learned to make, and Jack gave her plenty of opportunity to be heard … and, of course, she never argued with her mother-in-law.

Three

THE INLAND SEA
Rivers, Rhines and the Summer Lands

The first major attempt to drain the waters occurred in the twelfth century, when one of Britain's largest ecclesiastical settlements, Glastonbury Abbey, had outgrown the resources needed to feed its increasing population of monks and pilgrims. More land was needed.

From that time, the taming of the inland sea became a major occupation for the monks, who were set to work digging the drainage channels known as rhines. These water-filled ditches, some as large as rivers, gleam like silver threads across the levels. Criss-crossing the landscape like giant seams, they stitch together the fields and pastures coaxed from the tides.

This fragile landscape is now maintained by a complex system of sea defences, pumping stations and 'clyses', or sluice gates. In former times, tidal surges and winter rains covered vast areas of land that only reappeared during the summer months. These seasonal meadows, so welcome as extra pastures, were called the Summer Lands and gave the county of Somerset its name.

As the taming of the landscape continued, prosperity flourished amidst precarious conditions.

~ A Battle Most Unholy ~

If the elements did not themselves threaten this newly created, water-locked world, then people did. Disputes were frequent between the Church authorities and other landowners, and often took place between abbots and bishops. Skirmishes occurred that could hardly be described as Christian practice.

One famous case, illustrating centuries of rivalry between the abbots of Glastonbury and the bishops of Wells, even reached the Star Chamber for judgement. At the time, 1,500 acres of land on Wedmore were protected from floods by earth walls. These were deliberately breached by their Glastonbury neighbours, who stood by with weapons – including bows, arrows and billhooks – to shoot or strike down anyone who tried to prevent the ensuing flood.

Confronting this threat, the Wedmore faction repaired the damage – although that repair was instantly destroyed and new breaches made in five other parts of the wall.

The 'Glastonians' maintained that they had acted because their common grazing rights had been infringed by the 'Wedmorians' putting stakes and other obstacles in the way of their cattle. Nevertheless, the flooded party declared a state of emergency by ringing the Wedmore church bells and assembling the parishioners. They then announced that, if the walls were damaged again, 'the Abbot's men would be beaten and slain and fried in their own grease …'

Unsurprisingly, arbitration from the Star Chamber resulted not in suggestions of how to share, but in clearer demarcations of separation. When the new boundary-defining ditches had been dug, they became known as the olden or first enclosures.

*Archaeological remains preserved in the region's peaty waters show
that its earliest inhabitants lived in villages built on stilts amongst
the lakes and marshes. In recent years, an important archaeological find was made by a Mr Sweet whilst he was digging peat; he
found an ancient trackway consisting of planks or narrow logs
lashed together and raised above the water level, supported by a
cunning arrangement of pegs and poles beneath.*

*As water levels were always changing, it is believed that the
height of these tracks could be adjusted accordingly. It is thought
that laying them just below the surface of the water – where they
could still be used but not seen – contributed to the defence of the
region against later invasions. Only the locals, who knew where
they lay hidden in the dark peaty water, would have been able to
cross them.*

– LOSING THE BATTLE BUT NOT THE WAR –

It was towards the Somerset Levels that King Alfred fled,
defeated by the Danes who had captured his royal stronghold at
Chippenham, thereby occupying most of Wessex. Escaping his
pursuers, Alfred made his way by means of these secret paths to
the island of Athelney, the 'Isle of Princes', its access hidden in
the reeds and marshes. Here, two major rivers, the Parrett and
the Tone, once met in a wide expanse of water and swamp.

Legend tells us that soon after his defeat he was sheltered
by a poor local woman. It was a time of great uncertainty
and danger, and people knew not to ask too many questions.
Hiding in her reed hut, defeated and disheartened, King
Alfred's plight was worse than that of a beggar's. One day, as
his need to remain hidden confined him to the hut, she asked
him to keep an eye on the rough cakes that were baking in the
embers of her meagre fire while she worked elsewhere.

Alfred stared glumly at the fire with unseeing eyes, brooding over his difficulties and the plight of his kingdom. He didn't see the lick of flame, fanned by his sighs. He didn't smell the acrid smoke as the cakes burned to cinders. It was pain that brought him to his senses – as the goodwife returned and boxed his ears.

> Casn't thee mind the cakes, man? Dozzen thee zee 'em burn?
> I'm bound thee'l eat they vast enough as zoon as be thee
> turn!

Alfred made an abject apology, feeling even more useless than before. He explained that he had been preoccupied, and his hostess softened when she saw how distressed he was. She invited him to share his worries and Alfred told her what troubled him. When she realised that it was her king she had assaulted, she felt it was her turn to apologise, and Alfred drew both comfort and hope from her loyalty.

In time, he was joined by a small band of survivors and by a steady trickle of fighters still loyal to him. Alfred's secret resistance movement grew, despite there being a price on his head. On the Isle of Athelney, he built a fort and gathered his followers, and from there he sent his emissaries to ready the men of Wessex and beyond, biding his time, preparing to turn the tide.

King Alfred was an excellent harpist, and, disguised as a wandering minstrel, he would leave his hiding place and be wel-

comed into the Danes' camps. There, under the pretence of tuning his harp, he would eavesdrop on their battle plans, and then sing so sweetly that they never suspected he was anything other than a travelling musician. Never in the history of minstrelsy has a harp been tuned and retuned so often!

Athelney is the lowest-lying hill fort in Europe, its gentle slope hardly rising above sea level. Gratitude for the sanctuary that the island had given him prompted Alfred to have a monastery built there. This was accomplished in the days of peace, after the English victory at Ethandun and the conversion of the Danes' leader Guthrum to Christianity.

The winding River Parrett regularly floods, submerging the surrounding land in a vast and churning lake. Were it not for the menacing trace of its current, you would never guess that a river lay beneath the lake's seething waters. It is easy to believe the local legend which tells us that this river takes a human life every year — a man, a woman and a child in succession. Folklore describes how this river's malevolence can even possess willows, bending them to do its evil will. This happened one sad day, when a young woman stayed too late in Langport on the banks of the Parrett.

By the beds of green withies a young man I espied
Lamenting his true love, lamenting his bride.
All on a summer's morning she went to Langport town
But she never came home again, she never came home again
She never came home again when the moon it went down.
Oh Ellum do grieve and Oak he do hate, but Willow, Willow, Willow
Willow do walk if you travel late.
By the beds of green withies when morning did arise

He found his dear Nancy, all a-drownded she lies.
All on a summer's morning she went to Langport town
But she never came home again, she never came home again
She never came home again when the moon it went down.
Oh Ellum do grieve and Oak he do hate, but Willow, Willow,
Willow
Willow do walk if you travel late.
I've lost my dearest Nancy, he sobbed and he cried
Afloating down the river, all a-drift on the tide.

Despite being a managed waterscape since the Middle Ages, as recently as 1970 it was only possible to reach some homes in rowing boats and coracles, during times of flooding. Nearby is the village of Burrowbridge, where the Parrett is barely contained by the high banks, built not long after the events in the following story took place. Rising above the meanders, like a smoothed sugar loaf, looms Burrow Mump. Local legend tells us that it was built around a labyrinth winding through its hollow hill, and indeed its shape is so surprising in such a flat landscape that many assume – wrongly – that it was man-made ...

~ THE KING OF THE MOLES ~

As direct descendants of the family still live on the estate, I will not reveal its name, but, not so very long ago, the lands surrounding the Great House reached right down to the brooding and opaque waters of the River Parrett. The house, being on a rise, had always escaped the worst of the flooding, and a magnificent avenue of 200 ancient oak trees had kept the soil in place with roots so deep that they too had managed to withstand the strength of the floods.

The old lord had been respected and well-liked, mainly because he had kept himself to himself and never interfered.

If he had ever been outspoken enough to profess any motto, it would have been something like, 'Live and Let Live' or 'Let's not be Hasty'. When his beloved wife died in childbirth, leaving him an only son, the old lord became even more retiring. So, whilst he was alive, everything trundled on much as it had always done.

However, when he died and his son inherited the estate, things changed overnight. The young lord couldn't lay eyes upon anything without wanting to change it, and without demanding instant results. He showed no respect for weather, seasons, traditions or the laws of nature.

The head gardener was summoned and instructed to hire extra men to chop down those old-fashioned oak trees, whose leaves made such a mess in the autumn. The gardeners' disapproving mutterings were like the distant rumblings of thunder threatening an approaching storm. In three months, trees that had taken 300 years to grow were no more, and where their mighty network of roots had been there now lay craters of gaping earth.

This gave the new lord another idea: not only must the craters be filled in, but all the sloping lawns and water meadows to the riverbank must be levelled. This latest order drew outspoken protests from the head gardener and all the other servants.

'But Sir, what of the floods come autumn? That slope is the only thing between you and they, and now with the gurt trees gone the waters will lie deeper and longer on the land.'

The young lord would not see reason and the enormous task of levelling the ground began. Not a hole could be filled without the lord placing a billiard ball on the raw earth to see whether it rolled in any direction. Eventually, the vast, featureless expanse was planted with grass seed. The new grass sprang up and, one morning, the young lord looked out of the windows of the Great House, and all he could see was a flat green world in which it seemed that each and every blade of grass was pointing in the same direction. Had it not been for a few fluffy white clouds making the sky look untidy, all would have been perfect.

Earthly perfection lasted for the rest of that day, until he decided that the meanders of the river were rather an untidy shape, with their curling and wriggling like some giant worm. All would look far neater if the course of the river was changed into a nice straight line. Eventually this too was done, and the grass was replanted when the ground had passed the billiard ball test. Then the land was finally all as smooth and una-dorned as a billiard's table should be, with the line of the river providing the straight edge that any table requires. Had it not been for the breeze blowing unsightly ripples on the river's sur-face, all would have been perfect.

Earthly perfection lasted until the next morning, when the lord was horrified to see random dirty brown heaps dotted about his perfect lawn. The head gardener was summoned and an explanation demanded. Barely able to speak past his huge grin, the gardener said: 'Sir, they moby-warps is come.'

This was the country name for moles, and, though the young lord hadn't given a passing thought to the humble mole before, he could certainly see the damage they did to his smooth per-fection. When his fit of rage finally allowed him to speak, he gave the order for the gardener to have the creatures destroyed.

'Sir, you haven't asked for my advice and I'm not giving you any. What I am giving you is a warning – do not have me destroy they moby-warps. I've kept up with all this here nonsense this far, though its gone against my conscience, but now my conscience is bidding me to give you fair warning that if you persist in this, gurt harm will befall, even if I am the first gardener on God's Earth to speak up for those little varmints.'

Reason and sensitivity were not the young lord's strong points. He gave the order again, this time with threats, and the mole cull was on. So many moles were killed that soon the gardener added a moleskin wardrobe of trousers, gaiters, gloves, jackets, hats and slippers to his traditional moleskin waistcoat. His wife had moleskin caps and aprons, and moleskin dusters brought the shine on her windows up a treat. Still the moles kept coming, and soon hers was not the only baby on the estate to rejoice in the comfort of moleskin nappies. Then, just as the ladies of the congregation were debating whether to provide the parish church with a moleskin altar cloth, it seemed that the moles were no more.

The next morning, the young lord looked out over his desecrated lawn and saw that, although it was marred with flattened brown patches, no new crumbling heaps had appeared. With relief, he ordered the bare patches to be resown with grass seed, and within a few weeks his dream of perfection was restored – apart from an untidy flock of birds shifting about the lawn in search of worms in this mole-free expanse.

Perfection lasted until the next day, when huge heaps of shovelled earth appeared, each about twenty times the size of the previous ones. Foaming with fury, the young lord sent for the head gardener.

''Tis the King of the Moby-Warps, the King of the Moles to you Sir, who has heard his people are in distress and has come himself to see what he can do.'

'Well get rid of him, and be quick about it.'

'That, Sir, is beyond my wit and skill. There's only one man on God's Earth fit to catch the King of the Moles, and that man is Micky-the-Mole himself.'

'Then fetch him here immediately.'

'There's no fetching Micky-the-Mole, Sir, because he is one of the travelling people and he do go where he do go. Perhaps he may chance by in the autumn when the weather do close in.'

So that was that, and the young lord watched helplessly as, day by day, the King of the Mole's revenge changed his beautiful flat meadow into something resembling a lunar landscape. At last, with summer's end, the travelling people returned to their winter camp. The young lord was disconcerted one evening to have his study door flung open without the benefit of an announcement from his butler. There stood Micky-the-Mole, his long, prehensile nose whiffling the unaccustomed air of indoors and his huge hands dangling like a pair of shovels.

'I hear you wants to see me,' he said, without once looking at his future employer.

'Here you are at last. You are to get rid of the King of the Moles for me.'

'You gets nothing for nothing. What's in it for me?'

'A bag of gold if you capture the beast and show him to me.'

'Show me the size of the bag, and if it be gurt enough to stuff the creature in, it's a bargain.'

At last, Micky-the-Mole was satisfied with a bag as big as four potato sacks, and spat on the palm of his hand – which the young lord was obliged to shake to seal the deal.

Not long after, the young lord was sitting in his study with his curtains drawn against the woeful sight of his destroyed grounds, when he heard a horrendous heaving and scraping – and then the door was kicked open. There was Micky-the-Mole dragging a cage; in it was a mole the size of a calf. His huge paws had bent the bars and his claws had gouged ruts through the parquet flooring. A hiss of rage squeezed its way through the rows of jagged teeth as he caught the scent of his enemy. As for the young lord, he would have thought himself dreaming and in the grip of some monster-filled nightmare – if he had not seen the golden crown upon the animal's head, proving that he was truly in the presence of the Mole King.

'And now I want you to take him away and kill him.' So saying, he produced the bag of gold, which was placed on the top of the cage.

Just as Micky-the-Mole was dragging the cage away, the young lord called him back.

'And I don't want you to give him an easy, clean death. I want you to kill him in the slowest, most painful way possible, and come back tomorrow to tell me how he died.'

The torturer leered and dragged the scrabbling creature away. Next day he was back. 'I thought long and hard about the worst death I could muster,' he said, 'and it were no easy task to make up my mind. I thought to take him to where the river waxes tidal and leave him in his cage in the shallows, drowning slowly as the tide rises. But then I thought that would be too clean a death for him. I thought to set him in a ring of fire and build the fire up slowly, so he died burnt to death and tormented by the smell of his own scorched whiskers. But that would have been too warm and cosy a death for him. I thought of dropping him from one of the great cliffs of Cheddar Gorge, but that would have been too quick a death for him. By all the elements I was considering the best way for him to die …'

'Yes, yes,' cried the ever-hasty lord, salivating at these horrific possibilities. 'And which did you choose?'

'Having considered water, fire and air, I decided on the worst possible death – and so I buried him alive!'

The young lord let out a great sigh of satisfaction, and in a fit of unaccustomed generosity gave the torturer an extra bag of gold.

So yet again, once the grass seed had sprouted, earthly perfection reigned … Reigned for but a day, because on the morrow came a truly rainy day, followed by another and another; the rainy days were without number. Gone were the mature oak trees, the meanders and the slopes which would have channelled the flood waters away from the house. The head gardener watched furniture and carpets being washed away, and then the ancestral portraits and chandeliers. He watched and he waited, and it was not until the young lord was clinging to the roof of the Great House that the gardener appeared in his coracle to lift him off.

'I was thinking, Sir, that if someone had not ordered they moby-warp tunnels to be filled in, they would have been a pipe system like, to take all this nasty water away downstream ...'

On many a moonlit night, the head gardener would row upstream to Burrowbridge Mump, known locally as the 'King of the Moles' Castle'. There he would set his ear to the hollow hill and listen to the scrabbling of huge claws and Micky-the-Mole's harsh chuckle. Then he would hear the chink-chink of gold as the two friends counted their well-earned treasure.

Oh there's gentlefolk will swear by a stag in all his rights
For a hero on the heather he will be
And there's others swear the hare is the loveliest of sights
When she leaves her dewy form upon the lea.
But old moldiewarp he do work while he can
And he is the choice of the labouring man
Oh the hare and the stag is for them that likes to ride
But old moldiewarp's the choice for me.
Stag he waited and the pack had to turn and double back
Where old moldiewarp has been a-digging true
But a hare a-going round will be free of horse and hound
For the boldest rider dare not follow through.
But old moldiewarp turns a pasture into tilth
And he isn't afeared to work not he
Yes old moldiewarp turns a pasture into tilth
And he's not afeared to work not he.
Oh a pie of venison will very soon be done

And a hare that's jugged don't last an hour or so
But if you want some more you must take and hunt again
While old moldiewarp he harbours down below.
Oh old moldiewarp he can build a house he can
And he tunnels and he plasters very free
Yes old moldiewarp he can build a house he can
And he's not afeared to work not he.
So let others go a-hunting for their antlers by the score
For their pasties and their pies and fireside rug
But I've worn this moleskin weskitt now for twenty years
and more
And my moleskin cap do keep me warm and snug.
For old moldiewarp he wears velvet like a king
And he don't begrudge you take it if you can
Oh the hare and stag are both for those that like to ride
But old moldiewarp's the choice of the labour man.

Somerset is rather good at producing mud. Many have seen the revellers at the famous Glastonbury Festival covered all over with this pale glutinous uniform, closer fitting than any glove. At the end of the festival, hundreds of tents are dug out of the slime, their added coating having made them impossible to handle without thick gloves.

Mud has also been useful in providing more permanent accommodation, as it was essential to Somerset's brick manufacturing industry. The town of Bridgwater, near the Parrett estuary, grew rich on an abundance of this natural resource, and its bricks are distinguishable to this day by their strikingly orange hue.

Somerset's mud has been used for culinary purposes too – especially amongst the gypsy community, who are great storytellers …

⌐ WHEN THE GOOD LORD MADE THE ANIMALS ⌐

At the Rose and Crown Inn, in the village of Huish Episcopi, the local storyteller was holding forth. Today, Caspar-the-Clay was telling an ancient gypsy story about the origin of animals. He had been awarded this title because of his gypsy skill at baking hedgehogs in clay, his hedgehog roast being a local delicacy relished by a chosen few when the usual supplies of pheasant, hare and deer ran out. The following story's version of events might have horrified or amused any clergyman, as well as their famous adversary, Darwin.

But Caspar's audience was mesmerised. They followed every gesture of his skilful hands, whilst his warm voice smoothed the well-worn words of the tale told by countless generations. As he peeled back the layers of time, the audience was so entranced that Truth herself would have paused to listen …

Long, long ago, the Good Lord created this beautiful world in which we all live. Of course it was flat in those days, and how it got to be round is another story, which all goes to show that He didn't make everything all in one go. This world happened to be His favourite bit of Creation, and one day He decided to pay it a visit to see how it was getting on. So there He was, taking a stroll, admiring how the trees had grown, smelling the lovely perfume of the wild roses on the breeze and having a bathe in the ponds and a paddle in the streams. But all along He felt that something was not quite right. All day He delighted in the beauty of what He had made. He marvelled at the flaming colours of the sunset and the mysterious shades of the twilight. That night, He slept comfortably in some bracken – and it was just as well that it wasn't raining or this tale might never have started.

In the morning, He woke and realised what had been troubling Him. It was all too quiet! There was no singing of the birds at dawn, no rustling or scampering or pounding of hooves, no barks or bleats or calls – and that's because animals had not been made yet. So the Good Lord decided to make all the animals then and there, and liven things up.

He went down to the river – some say it must have been the River Parrett, on account of its bountiful quantity of mud – and started to take up great lumps of clay. Fortunately, it was low tide and there was plenty to hand. He started to make all the animals of the fields and the forests. He made all the beasts of the air and all those that live beneath the earth. He put the clay shapes on the riverbank and, when they were dry, He breathed upon them to give them life. And so they scampered and crawled and fluttered away.

The creatures of rivers and seas were placed into the Parrett's welcoming waters before they could dry out. A few swam upstream but most swam downstream to the open sea. From there, some made their way to the shores of other lands, some stayed in the ocean and some found other river mouths and swam against the current. Salmon and Eel could not make up their minds, and have been going to and fro between salt and sweet ever since.

All day long Our Lord worked, and at last was coming to the end of His labours. Evening came, and, with the setting of the sun, the mist began to rise from the river. There was just one last animal being made, still clay in Our Lord's hands, and it just so happened to be Hedgehog. As the air cooled, the Good Lord sneezed and Hedgehog came to life in His hands – but he hadn't been finished, so he scuttled away into the long grasses with no covering on him but his thin and wrinkly skin.

The Creator returned to his heavenly realm well satisfied with His work, as were all the animals – apart from Hedgehog. From the first moment, Hedgehog complained. You could hear him coming long before you could see him, snorting and grunting his complaints and making scornful remarks about the One who had made him. With no proper covering like all the other animals, he complained about being sunburnt in the summer and he complained about being frozen in the winter. The brambles and nettles tore and stung him, and he was always uncomfortable. The other animals made fun of his appearance and he became even more resentful. Hedgehog didn't have a good word to say about anyone and he didn't have a good word to say about himself. He had become impossible to live with.

The next time the Creator came to visit His favourite part of Creation, He was met by a delegation of animals who couldn't stand it any more.

'What was the point,' they wanted to know, 'in making such a beautiful place to live in and then making a creature like Hedgehog to spoil it?'

The animal sounds Our Lord had so longed for were now a cacophony of squeals, howls, bellows and derisive whistles, and He agreed that something had to be done. He announced that Hedgehog would be permitted to wander amongst the animals and borrow any coat or covering that he fancied, just to try it on for comfort, to help him choose whichever would be his for evermore. The noise subsided as all agreed that it was a fair and generous offer.

Hedgehog could hardly wait! Bear's coat was lovely and warm, but rather heavy and surely too hot for summer. Hedgehog returned it, and due to his nettle rash didn't notice Bear's fleas, which were now exploring their new home. He tried on Squirrel's coat, but decided that it would be too light for winter. It was returned without Hedgehog noticing Squirrel's fleas joyfully joining their cousins. Rabbit's coat would be just right for all seasons, but looked so dull. Surely he could do better than that. Hedgehog returned it – but not before Rabbit's fleas were making new friends and greeting long-lost relations.

Hedgehog found himself by a stream in which he noticed a silvery gleam. Fish scales would look stunning, but would soon become smelly out of water. Just then, Kingfisher darted across – and Hedgehog knew that what he wanted was feathers. Light in summer, fluffed out and warm for winter and oh, such gorgeous colours! Then, as Hedgehog remembered that he could choose from *any* animal, he decided that this also meant that he could choose from *every* animal. He asked for a coat made from the most colourful feathers of all the birds – and his request was granted.

Next day he found he was covered in a glossy array of every shade that could be seen in nature. Orange and blue from Kingfisher jostled with Woodpecker's green. The subtle hues of Owl and Sparrow and Dove vied with the brilliance of Yellowhammer, Starling and all the Finches. Behind him trailed Pheasant's brindled glory, and all was topped by a crest of Robin's rosiest red. This vision of loveliness stirred in the breeze, a shimmering chorus of colour.

As Hedgehog drifted daintily through the woods, all the other animals gasped in awe and bowed low before this splendid newcomer. At last they realised who this apparition was, but by then Hedgehog's little nose was tilting upwards with pride. Now he was expecting them to step aside if they met him on the woodland paths and to give up their food or resting places. His nose grew more pointed and tilted, his manner more superior and overbearing – and he was even more impossible to live with.

The next time Our Lord appeared on Earth, He was not best pleased to be met by an even angrier delegation.

'Leave it with me,' He promised.

Winter was coming and Hedgehog, in all his grandeur, had already evicted a family of weasels from their home to prepare his winter quarters. Squirrels, who should have been busy burying acorns, had been put to work carrying dry leaves to serve as bedding for his winter comfort.

With the first frost, Hedgehog was fast asleep, snoring through his little, pointy, upturned nose. His first dream wasn't a very pleasant one, and it went on for months because, as he was hibernating, he couldn't wake up from it. In his nightmare, Hedgehog dreamed that he was being turned inside out. Roll as he might amongst the leaves, he could not get away from this terrible dream until spring came; it was a relief to wake up.

It was full moon when Hedgehog left his bed and went looking for his first meal. He trotted along the woodland trails until he came to a large puddle. There, a most curious and ugly animal was staring up at him. Hedgehog hadn't seen anything so bizarre. If he hadn't felt quite certain of his standing, he might have been rather scared. He bent closer to look. Instead of retreating respectfully in the manner to which Hedgehog had become accustomed, the hideous creature drew closer. Well, Hedgehog was certainly not the one who was going to give way. He peered so close that his little pointy nose broke the skin of the water and the ugly stranger disappeared into ripples.

It was then that Hedgehog realised he had been staring at an image of himself. The terrible dream had come true and he really had been turned inside out. Those jagged spikes covering the nightmare creature were the quills of the feathers whose soft beauty had been reversed.

From that time to this, Hedgehog has been scuttling around even faster than before. That's because the feathers which are now on the inside are tickling him wherever he goes, and wherever he goes he is still complaining. Now he only comes out at night, in case the other animals remember how beautiful he used to be and make fun of his strange appearance. During his long winter sleep he dreams, hopefully, that one spring he will wake to find himself turned inside out again.

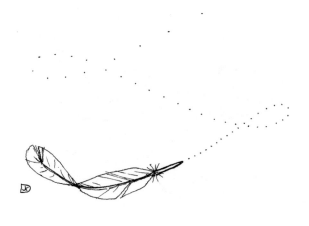

⌐ Yeovil's Giant Hay Thief ⌐

In the eighteenth century, on the outskirts of Yeovil, farmers discovered that their hay was being stolen from the haystacks in their fields. It looked as though an animal, rather than a person, was responsible, because of the way it had been pulled out in great tufts. However, so much was missing – and from so high up on the stacks – that nobody could think of any animal that could possibly be the culprit, unless it were a bear – and wild bears had not been seen in England for about 200 years.

The farmers clubbed together to offer a reward for the thief's capture, and some soldiers who were garrisoned at Yeovil decided to solve the mystery and claim the prize. As the thefts always occurred at night, they waited until dark to take up their positions near those haystacks that had been most recently despoiled. It was a moonlit night and they were confident of success.

The fields bordered the River Yeo, and one of the soldiers soon saw a huge, dark shape emerge over the bank and crawl across the water meadow towards a haystack. Frantically signalling to those in its path to stand aside, a couple of the soldiers shot it.

Great was their amazement to discover that it was an enormous eel. Doubtless it had grown so large that there was insufficient food in the river to sustain it, and, in its desperation, hay was better than nothing. It had been using its immense length to rear up towards the top of the stacks, where it could pull out mouthfuls more easily.

So great was the beast that it took eight draught horses to drag it back to the barracks, where a tree was felled for a spit, and the monster was roasted over two fires. Within an hour, every vessel in the neighbourhood was filled with the eel's fat and a search had to be made for more receptacles. When the soldiers returned with these, the grease was running through the cracks in the door and over the threshold.

People said that it must have been one of the giant eels that could be found on the Berrow Sandbank. It had probably swum upstream from the Parrett estuary, and, meeting the confluence of the Parrett and the Yeo at Langport, had continued to swim towards Yeovil.

There was so much eel to eat in the coming months that everyone grew tired of it, and even the dogs eventually refused it. The eel dripping sustained everyone throughout the winter, providing fuel for the lamps (bright, if rather smelly), and proving to be a marvellous medicine, an ointment that cured chilblains and the rheumatics.

⁓ ELI'S EEL ⁓

Nobody knew what had possessed Eli Boswell to choose a pet eel as his closest companion; even harder to understand was the fact that the animal seemed to return his affection.

Every February, Eli would go fishing for eels in the River Parrett, when they came home at last after their long swim all the way from the Sargasso Sea, some 3,500 miles away. They would be rather hungry after their journey and quite incapable of resisting the baited ball of knotted wool that he cast into the river. As the delightful taste of rotten fish was carried through the water, the eels would try to force themselves through the entangled threads to get at the bait. Even when it was swept out of the water they were still clinging to it, like a writhing, squirming, slippery knot of shining threads. Only when they noticed that they had left the protection of the water and were swinging through the air, would they let go. Eli's many years of practice ensured that, at this critical moment, he had their heaving mass positioned above the old tin bath that he had borrowed from Farmer Lynch – it was certain that Eli himself never used a bath on any other occasion.

Before long, the tin bath was so full that it was useless to carry on, as many eels were escaping by using the backs of their fellow prisoners to reach the rim of the bath. Eli used to say that when the bath had been emptied, with the eels sold off in buckets, he would settle down to enjoy a smoke. One day, reaching into his pocket, he discovered that his pipe was rather wetter and more flexible than usual, and he drew out the little eel whom everyone was soon to know as Edward – and no jokes about smoked eel were ever permitted when he explained how Edward and he had found each other.

So Edward would go wherever Eli would go, travelling in his pocket in the comfort of a twist of moistened grass. He was a great favourite in their local, the Rose and Crown at Huish Episcopi; as Eli quaffed his pint, Edward would sip whatever his friend was having from a champagne flute. The sight of these two became quite an attraction, and Eli was soon pleased to discover that visitors were continually buying him pints so that he could tip some into Edward's glass, and they could see an eel drinking beer in a pub with their own eyes.

Time passed and Edward grew. He was now too big to fit into Eli's pocket and was worn as a belt. The two friends increased together in both size and affection – Edward due to lack of exercise as he was being carried everywhere instead of sveltely swimming, and Eli because he was downing an unprecedented quantity of beer. It was when Edward had become so large that he had to be wrapped twice around Eli's new beer belly, that the two friends had their first tiff.

One night in the Rose and Crown, Edward decided that he had outgrown his champagne flute and took a sip from Eli's tankard. There was a shocked intake of breath shared by all who witnessed the occurrence. That eel had got above his station – and Eli refused to let him have any more beer. In a huff, Edward reared up from the table, slithered onto the floor, wrapped himself round a few spaniels – nearly squeezing them to death from temper on his way out – and went to sulk in the ditch.

After that, no more liberties were taken with another man's drink, and, following a period of good behaviour, Edward was promoted to using a wineglass.

The two companions lived happily together and were the talk of the county, with people coming from far and further to see them. Edward was now too big to be carried and would slither along beside his friend like a dog at (h)eel. It was he who was the first to shuffle off this mortal coil – quite literally, in his case.

Eli being a thrifty man, or maybe because he just wanted to remain close to his friend, made a pair of braces out of Edward's skin. These eel-skin braces were worn rain or shine, and whenever it was suggested that his visits to the pub were too frequent, he would have the perfect explanation: he often tried to pass the Rose and Crown – with no intention at all of entering – when he would be brought up short by a tug from his braces, a pull so violent that he was powerless to resist, leaving him no option but to obey …

In a later and more regimented age, eel fishing became the subject of a range of restrictions, either to fit in with EU regulations or to prevent overfishing. An army of inspectors often seemed to be at hand, patrolling the riverbank looking for tell-tale tin baths, with stiff fines following accordingly.

Locals therefore took to eel fishing with open umbrellas lying upturned in the mud, in which to empty their catch. In time, these too aroused the inspectors' suspicions – particularly when it was actually raining. On these occasions, the eel fishers would seize their umbrellas and hold them in the expected fashion, whilst ignoring the fact that it suddenly appeared to be raining eels …

> Eely Pie, Eely Pie, a penny a pocketful buy, buy, buy
> They catch them in buckets they catch them in nets
> They catch them in fistfulls and fill up their hats
> Eely Pie, Eely Pie, a penny a pocketful, buy, buy, buy

Four

THE CURVED HORIZON
Hills and Moors

Somerset is the only county in Britain that boasts five ranges of hills. Perhaps because so much of it is flat, or used to be underwater, any reach of higher ground has particular significance. Admittedly, Somerset shares the Blackdown Hills with Devon, but otherwise it claims the Quantocks, Poldens, Brendons, and the Mendips for its own.

In 1956, the Quantocks were designated as England's first Area of Outstanding Natural Beauty. The poets Coleridge and Wordsworth, who delighted in rugged landscapes, came to live there. From his cottage in Nether Stowey, Coleridge wrote one of his most famous works, *The Rime of the Ancient Mariner*. A statue of this character was recently erected on the quayside at Watchet, where the hills give way to the Bristol Channel near Quantoxhead, believed to be the setting that first inspired the poem.

The old lady in the following story, however, had never strayed more than three miles from her native village of Crowcombe, which nestles in the Quantock Hills …

As I went over Quantock, as I went over Quantock
As I went over Quantock when I was very small
I couldn't get up they Quantocks, I couldn't get up they
Quantocks

I couldn't get up they Quantocks I couldn't get up at all.
As I went over Quantock, as I went over Quantock
As I went over Quantock and took my love with me
We danced along the Quantocks, we danced along the
Quantocks
We danced along the Quantocks from Buncombe to the sea.
Now I want to get up they Quantocks, I want to get up
they Quantocks
I want to get up they Quantocks along of me gurt old stick
I cassn't get up they Quantocks, I cassn't get up they
Quantocks
I cassn't get up they Quantocks, but I come down very
quick.

~ THE DRAGON OF SHERVAGE WOOD ~

Every September, the old lady would climb up into the hills
around Crowcombe to pick whortleberries. These she baked
into tarts that she sold at the Triscombe Revel fair.

Some said that those tarts were bewitched or 'overlooked',
because you couldn't eat one, with its dollop of cream, without going back for a second. After the second you were under
some strange compulsion to eat a third and so it went on, until
merciful release came when others in the same position had
ensured that none remained. In just one day at the fair, the old
lady managed to earn enough to pay a year's rent.

It was a terrible calamity for her, therefore, when a dragon
took up residence in Shervage Wood, her favourite place for
gathering whortleberries.

Like most dragons, it had started life eating the smaller animals, and, as it grew, it had progressed to eating sheep, cattle
and horses. Now that most of these had gone, humans were no

longer safe, even though it meant spitting out an extra skin —
and bundles of empty, charred clothes were all that remained
of a squire or two.

This particular mellow September day, the old lady sat at the
foot of the hill, fair dizzy with the juicy scent of whortleberries
'so ripe as a maiden's blush', as she said to herself. She didn't
know how to go about collecting them, for fear of the dragon.
Just then, she noticed dust rising from the road. Someone was
approaching — and as he neared she was delighted to see that he
was a stranger.

As he drew close she set to crying, alternating between rubbing her eyes and throwing her apron over her head. Of course
the stranger asked her what was wrong; peeking at him from
time to time from beneath dry eyelids, she could tell from the
axe in his belt that he was a woodcutter.

He told her that he was from Stogumber, all of three miles
distant, and on his way to Triscombe Revel, hoping to hire himself out to some nearby estate. When he mentioned Triscombe
Revel, the poor woman renewed her sorrows. On hearing that

she was now too old to climb into the hills, the kind woodcutter readily agreed to gather whortleberries for her. After all, what did she have to lose other than the basket with the firkin of cider, and hunks of bread and cheese, that she supplied to sustain him?

The woodcutter climbed up the hill and through the wood, noting the profusion of berry bushes in the clearings and the plentiful timber worthy of his axe. He had decided to make his way to the top of the hill and work his way downwards, picking as he went. At the top of a slope he decided to get started, but realised that he would need to empty the basket first, so he decided to have an early lunch. As it was such a hot day, the cider would be especially welcome.

He selected a huge log as his seat. Being half-covered by ferns, it took a few moments to make out the girth of this mighty piece of timber. Settling himself down, he drank thirstily from the firkin, and bit into the cheese. For a moment, the log seemed to stir beneath him. The woodcutter put it down to having drunk the cider too quickly on such a hot day. He took a few more swigs to steady himself, but this had no effect on the log. He definitely felt a rippling and then a creeping motion beneath him. He had sat on the sleeping dragon that the old lady had somehow failed to mention.

Still unaware of his fatal mistake, and outraged that a piece of wood should behave so unnaturally with one deemed an expert, he leaped to his feet and grabbed his axe.

'Do 'ee dare to move as I do chew me vittles, do 'ee?' exclaimed the outraged woodcutter, chopping into the trunk with such a mighty blow that it was split into two. As blood spurted out rather than wood chips, he looked more carefully, and could now discern two halves of a rather subdued dragon shuffling off in opposite directions.

His peace irretrievably disturbed, he downed the remaining picnic and set to work gathering whortleberries. Soon the basket and his hat were full, and he returned to the old woman, who thanked him warmly.

'Now I be so happy as a daisy in spring.'

'I were never told there be a gurt dragon up there in they woods.'

'Dost 'ee never know that? I thought every soul in Quantocks be knowing that!'

'What? Even when I told 'ee I were from Stogumber! Well, 'ee can tell folk there be two dragons now sithee.'

As the two dragon halves had shuffled off in opposite directions, they were too busy looking for each other to prey on the local fauna. And if the front part had managed to swallow something, where would it have ended up? As one part had moved in a westerly direction, and the other in an easterly, it would be some time before they found each other. They are searching still, and locals will tell you that they don't only close gates to secure livestock, but also to prevent their dragon from joining up again.

Wort pie, wort pie, come and buy my wort pie
Penny a little one, tuppence a big,
Sixpence a tart as round as your wig

Whortleberries, the Somerset name for bilberries, are still picked in the Quantocks and on Exmoor for tarts, jams and chutneys. At the Somerset County Cricket ground in Taunton, the tradition persists of making a giant whortleberry tart over 3ft across whenever the Australian cricket team is visiting. During the Second World War, women and boys would be paid by the bucketful to collect whortleberries, which were then used to dye the fabric for RAF uniforms. One old lady gleefully told me that it was common practice to add water to the berries to make them swell, so that fewer were needed to fill a bucket!

~ THE 'FIRST' HEDGEHOG ~

Not so long ago, two friends were lost in the Brendon Hills, having strayed three miles from their village. They came upon an object hidden in some undergrowth that they didn't recognise. For some time, they argued about whether it was animal or vegetable. At last, one persuaded the other that it was the overgrown casing of a giant sweet chestnut. At that point it unrolled and scuttled away. They gave chase – whereupon it curled itself up again and they couldn't tell which end was which, or whether it had a front or back end at all.

Nothing is more likely to arouse interest than two people staring intently at the ground. Soon they were joined by others, all equally helpless at identification. Eventually, someone remembered that in the next village there lived a man so ancient that he must be truly wise. He was so old that he hadn't spoken for over ten years and neither had he stirred – except to drink rum or smoke tobacco. People came from all over the county to behold this marvel, and were well satisfied when he accepted their offerings and they saw him move (rather like the not-yet-invented automata on Weston-super-Mare's pier). They decided to bring this old man the strange object, to see whether it would provoke him into breaking his years of silence.

There was an immediate difficulty with this plan, as no one could lift – let alone carry – it, without being scratched and prickled. Furthermore, whenever the bravest approached they were enveloped by swarms of fleas, which awed them into saying: 'That is a fearsome thing for to prickle and bite from afar!'

Some hours later, another brilliant plan was arrived at. As nobody could move the mysterious heap, the ancient would have to be brought to it. So he was trundled along in a wheelbarrow. The old man, still and silent, stared fixedly at it. Eventually, someone remembered to prime the pumps by administering the usual elixirs. Revived, he leant forward and pointed – and the silence of years was broken:

'Well I'll be blowed if I know what that be! Turn I round! Wheel I back!'

When they had pushed the old man home, they decided that this event should be commemorated. The blacksmith was commissioned to make a weathervane depicting the main characters, and with due ceremony it was installed on the roof of the nearest barn. There it remained for many a year, until it was struck by such a bolt of lightning that the barn was burned to the ground.

It is to be hoped that all the nearby hedgehogs escaped being roasted.

The most famous hill in Somerset, and some would say in the whole of Britain, is Glastonbury Tor. This extraordinary natural outcrop remained while the softer rocks around it were gradually eroded and their layers were washed away into the tides of Somerset's inland sea.

From the time when people first came to the Tor, they formed stories about this unique and magical place. Long after their creators were gone, the legacies of their tales remained. Deposits of legends built up layer by layer, formed over thousands of years by the comings and goings of race, language and religion.

Archaeological finds from the Tor include a ritual Neolithic axe, and a cache of fossils in the remains of a Romano-Celtic temple located beneath a church dedicated to St Michael, whose tower can still be seen today.

— GWYN AP NUDD —

Long, long ago, before people were divided into those who spoke Welsh and those who spoke English, the old gods were not just remembered but also revered, and Gwyn ap Nudd was worshipped at Glastonbury Tor.

A son of one of the gods of light, he was honoured particularly for bringing light into the dark places. He could be seen in the gleam on the dark waters of the rivers Severn and Thames. He could be seen in the distant sparkle of the Milky Way. His festival fell on May Day, a day of rejoicing for the people as it marked the return of their summer, when the hours of light outnumbered those of the dark.

Gwyn walked between the worlds of the light and the dark, bearer of the dead to the Other World.

From the East to the North
I am the escort to the grave
I have been where the soldiers of Britain were slain

He was the cause of a terrible battle in which he allowed the forces of darkness that he lived so closely with to consume his actions. Gwyn had a beloved sister, Creiddylad, who was a goddess of the land. When the noble knight Gwythr became betrothed to Creiddylad, Gwyn was jealous. He thought that Gwythr was not sufficiently highborn as there was no divine blood in him, and most of all he wanted to keep her for himself. Gwyn abducted Creiddylad, and her fiancé was compelled to attempt to rescue her by force.

But Gwyn was a mighty warrior: had he not been King Arthur's right-hand man in the hunt for a monstrous boar and the slaying of an undefeatable giant? Gwythr too had taken part and distinguished himself in those adventures, but now Gwyn fought his former companion-in-arms with unequalled savagery.

Capturing one of his rival's chieftains, instead of keeping his prisoner alive and asking for a ransom – as was the custom – he murdered him. Gwyn then forced the prisoner's son to eat his father's heart, and the young man lost his reason after being made to participate in this atrocity. Apart from the deed itself, the implication of this horrific act was not lost on Gwythr – the name of his beloved, Creiddylad, means 'heart'.

King Arthur was appealed to as a mediator. The hero whose path Gwyn had smoothed would now become his judge.

Arthur decided that the two warriors would fight over Creiddylad every May Day, each taking turns to win her companionship for six months. He also decreed that the fight would be renewed on the same day of each year until Judgement Day. Gwyn's punishment was to be banished to the other world – the underworld – the place of darkness beneath Glastonbury Tor, for half the year.

If this is a story about the struggle between summer and winter's dominion over the Earth, then it seems that King Arthur is still being obeyed to this day. With the passage of time, Gwyn's punishment included being demoted from pagan divinity by the Christian King Arthur to a lesser role – that of King of the Fairies, the magical folk who live under the hill.

> From the torment of battle,
> Fairy am I called,
> Gwyn the son of Nudd

– St Collen and the King of the Fairies –

The man whom we now know as St Collen had once been a mighty soldier, chosen by the Pope himself to pursue his Holy Wars. However, as he reached mature years, he turned from skill at arms to the skills of the mind. Still hale and hearty and already well travelled, he journeyed even further in pursuit of learning. At last he returned to these shores and soon became known as a distinguished scholar.

St Collen came to Glastonbury Abbey and rose to become its abbot in only three months. However, try as he might, this exalted position gave him no job satisfaction as he never seemed able to sufficiently improve people's behaviour. He therefore set himself a harder task, which was to wander the country as a missionary for some years. When he returned to his duties at the abbey, he discovered that things had gone from bad to worse.

The monks had returned to their undisciplined ways, just as though they had never received the benefits of his teaching.

Disheartened at how little effect he seemed to be having on his fellow men, he decided that life in a powerful position was not for him. He made himself a rocky cell in the lee of the great slopes of Glastonbury Tor and became a hermit. His life was now steeped in solitary contemplation and prayer. However, his peace was not to last long. Whilst meditating in his cell, he overheard the following conversation:

'They do say that this Tor be the King of the Fairies' castle.'

'Do they now?'

'They do indeed. The palace of Gwyn ap Nudd, King of the Fairies, lies beneath our feet in all its splendour ...'

This was too much for St Collen, who interrupted with: 'Silence with your pagan nonsense! 'King of the Fairies' indeed! Those 'fairies' are nothing but the spawn of the Devil, banished back to the dark where they belong by good King Arthur himself!'

But the first speaker was not going to take his reprimand meekly. His reply was a warning, maybe even a threat: 'Do you look to yourself, whoever you are; Gwyn ap Nudd will not take kindly to your belittlings.'

The following day, St Collen had a visitor: a messenger from Gwyn ap Nudd, commanding him to attend the Fairy King on the top of the Tor the next noon. St Collen did not obey the summons and, all through the next night, his cell was surrounded by the sound of sinister whisperings, in which no words could be distinguished, although they were loud enough. The tormented St Collen realised that madness lay in trying to make out what the voices were saying, and he tried to keep the voices from his mind with his prayers.

Gwyn ap Nudd's messenger returned on the morrow, hoping that St Collen had passed a good night and summoning him to meet the king at noon. This the saint did not do, and that night his cell was surrounded by the sounds of wailing and weeping – so loud that he could barely hear his own voice chanting prayers to keep the others at bay.

Again the messenger returned with the same solicitous remarks about the saint's rest and the same terse command. Again St Collen refused to obey. That night, the noises around his cell were horrendous beyond imagining and the hermit shook to his marrow with fear.

The next day, just before noon, he put a bottle of holy water in his pocket and started to climb the steep slopes of the Tor. To his amazement, when he reached the top there was no church, but a splendid palace with pennants flying in the breeze and countless servants rushing about wearing a splendid livery of blue silk down one side and red silk down the other.

Gwyn ap Nudd came to personally welcome his guest, and conducted him to a sumptuous banqueting hall where the most lavish of feasts was laid out, surpassing anything St Collen had ever seen – even when he had been in the service of the Pope. He gazed in wonder at the salvers of peacock tongues, the roast swans and the miniature castles made from marzipan. But when Gwyn ap Nudd invited him to eat, St Collen looked at him with a cold eye and said, 'Why would I wish to eat withered leaves?' Perhaps he was remembering all the cautionary folk tales of never eating fairy food if you ever wanted to leave Fairyland; perhaps he knew that the glamour of fairy wealth always turned into dry leaves; or perhaps he just didn't want to appear impressed.

Still smiling graciously, the king replied, 'In that case, tell me what you think of my servants. Are they not splendidly turned out?'

Now, St Collen knew very well what the holy teaching said – that in Hell, the souls of the wicked were condemned to both burn and freeze at the same time – so he replied, 'And why would I admire the red fire and the blue ice of Hell itself?' And with that, he took the bottle of holy water from his pocket and threw its contents over the company.

There was a great bang and a flash. When St Collen took his hands from his ears and dared to open his eyes, the king with all his retinue and the beautiful palace had disappeared. The Tor looked just as it usually did, with its little church and its cattle-cropped grass.

St Collen was never again troubled by Gwyn ap Nudd, who it was said had been …

… placed over the devils in the Other World
lest they destroyed the present race

Centuries later, in 1275, the church dedicated to St Michael at the top of the Tor was destroyed by an earthquake. People said that this was another attempt by Gwyn ap Nudd to regain his former kingdom. If so, the attempt was unsuccessful, as the church was replaced by another, also dedicated to St Michael.

So it was that one of the old gods was demoted to King of the Fairies and lastly to guardian of the imps in Hell, never to rise again, unless it be in story.

The trees a-turn yellow and so do the fallow, 'tis Michaelmas now.
Then glory to God and St Michael,
Who fights with the devil on the hill.
And singen we so merrily, with all good will: 'tis Michaelmas tide

— THE BIRTH OF ST BRIDGET —
AND HER MISSION IN GLASTONBURY

Bridget's mother was a slave woman – a Christian of English origin – who was a captive in a noble Irish household. Her owner was related to the royal house, and was possibly also a Druid. He fell in love with his slave, and his wife became very jealous. When the slave became pregnant, his wife insisted that she be moved on. As a Druidic prophecy stated that the woman would give birth to 'another Mary, mother of the Great Lord', this further fuelled her jealousy.

Under mounting pressure from his wife, Bridget's father gave the slave away to a colleague who was both a Druid and a bard. However, he stipulated that the child be returned to him as soon as it was born. The Druid agreed to this condition, and, soon after he had returned home with the pregnant slave, he received a visitor. This was the Queen of Ireland herself, who had heard that there would soon be a royal birth and wanted the Druid to prophesy about the child's future.

The Druid's enigmatic reply was: 'Happy the child born neither in nor out of the house.'

No amount of cajoling could get him to say anything else on the matter and the Queen had to be satisfied with that. As soon as she had left, the heavily pregnant slave returned from the byre, having finished the milking. She was carrying a pail of milk on her head, and, as she was about to step over the threshold, she was seized with labour pains. Baby Bridget was born on the threshold, and was bathed in the fresh milk that her mother naturally spilled in the process.

The child was returned to her father, and news of this strange birth had preceded her. As she grew up, her father gave her her own herd of cows, which Bridget loved to tend. Although her father knew St Patrick well, he had never consented to convert to Christianity. Despite this, Bridget herself was a devout Christian, which her father tolerated. However, she used to anger him by giving away much of their produce to the poor.

One day, when he was visiting the King of Leinster, he left her sitting in his chariot, with his sword. Just as he happened to be complaining to the King about her over-generous habits, she gave his sword away to a passing beggar, as she had nothing else at hand to give him. When she was presented to the King, who happened to be a Christian, he saw her remarkable religious potential and, despite her father's anger, took her part, even replacing her father's sword with his own!

As she grew older, she was increasingly recognised by bishops and kings as having a special spiritual grace, and she ran several religious settlements in Ireland. In time, she used her influence to gain her mother's freedom, and with her father's blessing the two women returned to the land of her mother's birth. They made their way to Glastonbury, and Bridget founded a religious settlement near the Tor, at Beckery. The name 'Beckery' comes from early Irish and means 'little Ireland', in reference to the many saints and missionaries who crossed the sea to settle and work in Somerset.

Her nuns were famous for the butter and cheeses they made, and for their acts of charity. Their herd had the reputation of being the best in all the land.

Bridget has always been strongly associated with cows and milk. On the tower of St Michael's Church, on top of the Tor, St Bridget is depicted in a now sadly eroded carving, seated on a stool whilst milking. Some say that the church was built in that place following the tradition of allowing a cow to wander until it came to rest, and building a shrine wherever that spot happened to be.

Her feast day falls close to the ancient Celtic festival of Imbolc, in early February, which celebrates the ewes producing milk in readiness for the lambing season. It is said that wherever Bridget milked a cow, for every drop milked a snowdrop grew.

Perhaps it is due to the prophecy that she would become 'another Mary, mother of the Great Lord' that she was reputed to be Jesus' foster mother when he was, according to local belief, brought to Glastonbury by his uncle. Although it is harder for us to accept this with our better-informed sense of history – as Bridget lived nearly 500 years later – it was a strongly surviving tradition until the middle of the 1900s.

– Joseph of Arimathea and the Holy Grail –

And did those feet in ancient time
Walk upon England's mountains green
And was the Holy Lamb of God
On England's pleasant pastures seen

Joseph of Arimathea was Jesus' uncle. Known and respected in the West Country as a wealthy tin merchant, he had

connections with both British royalty and the Roman admin-
istration in Palestine, where there was a high demand for his
tin.

Legend tells us that the young Jesus accompanied him on
his trading voyages. After their long journey from the ports of
Acre or Caesarea in the Eastern Mediterranean, they would at
last reach the Cornish tin mines, where their ships would be
loaded with ingots. On their return, they would hug the north
coast, sailing past Devon and into the Severn Sea (now known
as the Bristol Channel). From there they would make their way
inland along one of its many estuaries, sailing on Somerset's
inland sea as far as Glastonbury.

They would disembark at nearby Pilton, a name derived
from Pool Town ('pool' being the ancient word for harbour).
Pilton still commemorates these visits on its church's cer-
emonial banner. There, Joseph is depicted standing in a boat
holding his staff, with the young Jesus seated beside him. This
tradition is also remembered in a folk song:

Oh Joseph came a-sailing all over the sea
A-trading of metal, a-trading came he.
And he made his way to Mendip with our dear young Lord.
Oh Joseph, Joseph, Joseph was a tinner was he.
Oh Joseph came a-sailing all over the sea
A-seeking of metal all a-trading came he.
And away he went a-walking with our dear young Lord
Oh Joseph, Joseph, Joseph was a tinner was he

Some say that they also travelled overland for the last stage of
their journey, as in the words of this local nursery rhyme:

Oh Joseph was a tinner
He sailed his little boat

He came ashore at Watchet
'Cos he couldn't keep afloat

From Watchet, they made their way across the Quantocks by a path known as the Lord's Path (where exactly this route lay is now sadly lost), before at last reaching the Mendip Hills and Glastonbury.

Jesus' adult life was spent in the Holy Land, and it is not until after his death that his uncle Joseph played a significant role in the spiritual development of Britain.

After the crucifixion, Joseph of Arimathea's life was in danger. He was known to Pontius Pilate and had spoken out against Jesus' punishment. He had even assisted at Jesus' funeral rites and donated his own tomb for his burial.

One version of events tells us that he was consequently imprisoned and that as he lay incarcerated, Jesus appeared to him holding the drinking vessel that had been used for the wine at the Last Supper. He exhorted his uncle to take the cup and to hide it in a safe place until such time as it could work its influence.

Another version tells us that after the Last Supper, Joseph kept the chalice and used it to collect Jesus' blood during his crucifixion. Fearing persecution, and determined to keep this sacred vessel safe, he made his way to the distant but familiar land of Somerset. There, believing in the teaching of Jesus and in the Resurrection, he buried the cup at the foot of Glastonbury Tor, on the threshold of what was considered to be the entrance to the Other World.

A spring then burst forth, with waters of a markedly red colour, and this miraculous occurrence was of course linked to the red of the wine and the red of Jesus' blood. This spring still exists, gushing a minimum of 25,000 gallons of water a day as it flows in the heart of the Chalice Well Gardens. It is so rich in iron that it coats every surface with a glowing red deposit, giving it the apt name of the 'Red Spring'. This healing spring continues to be a site of pilgrimage, visited by people from all over the world.

In the Victorian era it was partially forgotten, visited only by local people for cures, but it was rescued from obscurity by a remarkable visionary, Wellesley Tudor Pole …

As a child, he had seen 'the colours of the prayers' rising during church services, and as a young man he had a vision of himself living as a monk in Glastonbury centuries earlier. Later, while serving in the Intelligence Corps during the First World War, he found himself in the Judean Hills, near Joseph of Arimathea's birthplace. It was there, lying wounded in hospital, that he conceived the idea of a 'minute's silence' – the moments of quiet which became, during and after the Second World War, the Silent Minute. From 10 November 1940, with the support of Winston Churchill, King George VI and the BBC, the nation began to observe the Silent Minute every night at 9 p.m., as the bells of Big Ben chimed. The minute of silence, to pray or meditate for freedom and peace, was observed throughout the country, on land and sea, in air-raid shelters and hospitals, on battlefields and in private homes.

In 1945, when a British Intelligence officer asked a high-ranking Nazi official why he thought Germany had lost the war, the Gestapo officer replied that he thought it was because of the Silent Minute: it had been a potent weapon that they didn't understand, and for which there had been no counter-measure.

Chalice Well Gardens has since become a World Peace Garden, one of a growing network that aims to reach across the globe.

A few feet away from the Red Spring flows the 'White Spring', whose calcite deposits used to produce lacy curtains of stalactites; these were sadly destroyed when a reservoir was built around the spring in 1872. Even at that time there was a public outcry, as these magical waters seeped throughout the combe, covering its pools and vegetation with a coating of twinkling white crystals, a vision worthy of Fairyland. Indeed, the caverns and passages that the spring had carved beneath the Tor were believed to lead to one of the entrances to the King of the Fairies' realm. One of the objections to building the reservoir was that it would destroy the archaeological remains of the earliest monks' cells in the area.

After Joseph had buried the chalice, he asked to be given some land on which to found a settlement for practising Jesus' teachings. King Arviragus gave him what became known as the 'Twelve Hides of Glastonbury', small islands or areas of land around the Tor which could be relied upon to escape the seasonal rise and fall of the inland sea. Other versions of this story say that Joseph was given these twelve parcels of land, each measuring some 160 acres, in recognition of the twelve companions who had made the journey with him to Glastonbury, just as the twelve disciples had accompanied Jesus.

It was against the protective slope of the Tor that one of the earliest buildings dedicated to Christian worship arose. Made of humble wattle-and-daub, it preceded the great churches of the East – Coptic and Orthodox – by centuries. Indeed, archaeology places it amongst the first churches in the world.

At least 500 years after the chalice was first hidden, the time that Jesus had predicted to his uncle finally arrived: in the reign of King Arthur, those Knights of the Round Table who were without sin saw a vision of this sacred vessel. Since medieval times it has been referred to as the Holy Grail, and the stories of the search for it are amongst the most enduring of European romances.

— KING ARTHUR AND THE TOR —

King Arthur was haunted by the memory of a terrible wrong, a crime that he himself had committed even whilst being respected and lauded by courtiers and commoners alike. The King, whilst fighting for justice, chivalry and the protection of the weak, was a murderer – a murderer of his own son and a mass murderer of countless newborn baby boys – just like a certain infamous king before him.

Arthur had learned, to his horror, that he had unknowingly made love to his own half-sister, and that she had conceived his child; this was how it had come about:

Arthur hadn't seen Morgaine since she was a little girl. She had been leading a secluded life, training to become one of the 'Nine Sisters', the priestess custodians of the Isle of Avalon, sanctuary and gateway to the Other World. When she had come to court, a fully grown woman, beautiful and alluring, he hadn't recognised her. Neither had he known that as well as being his half-sister, she was also an enchantress. With her magical powers, it had not been difficult for her to seduce Arthur – indeed, in certain circles she was known as Morgaine-le-Fey, Morgan of the fairy folk.

Through her magic arts, Morgaine had discovered that, because of his wife's betrayal, Arthur's marriage would be cursed with barrenness – i.e. Guinevere's adulterous affair with his favourite knight, Sir Lancelot, meant that she and Arthur would never be blessed with a child. Theirs was no longer a Sacred Marriage, and Morgaine, Priestess of the Sacred Land, knew that the land would be unforgiving. Some say that this is why she resolved to conceive Arthur's child – for the good of the land – so that there might be an heir to all that her brother had accomplished, and that all would not be torn apart by war and treachery at Arthur's death.

Others say that her motive was simply one of revenge. Morgaine believed that Arthur's father, Uther, had murdered hers so that he could seize her mother for himself. The story went that Arthur's father had done this with the help of the wizard Merlin; perhaps he had even been Merlin's tool, made to believe that it was his own desire all along. But if Merlin had secret arts, so did she – and as she grew up, she had schemed and waited for the right moment to pitch her arts against his. Just as Merlin had helped to destroy her father in order to raise up his own man, so she would bring down that man's son.

When Arthur learned that he had slept with his own sister, he was consumed with shame. And when he learned that a son had been born, he dreaded the incest coming to light and the further shame that would follow. This fear was so overwhelming, it overcame any qualms he may have felt at the thought of murdering an innocent child. But how was the boy to be found? How could he be identified? The only sure way was to have all male infants of the right age put to death. Arthur gave the order for them all to be found, placed in a boat and cast adrift, to perish at sea.

So it was that Arthur was being eaten away by guilt, a guilt that he could share with no one. He went through the motions of giving his blessing to the Knights of the Round Table as they went forth on their quests. He gazed with unseeing eyes at Guinevere and Lancelot as their liaison threatened to drive a wedge through his court and bring destruction to his realm. His wife did not invite him to share his troubles; her own guilt prevented her from seeing the haunted look in his eyes. His beloved Lancelot did not ask what troubled his friend and king – he thought he already knew the answer.

And so the weary days dragged by, with Arthur gradually losing faith in himself and what he stood for.

One evening, a holy sister from a nearby community came to the court begging for alms. She had come to ask the King for money to extend St Bridget's settlement at Beckery, close to Glastonbury Tor. Arthur received her warmly and promised her the funds she needed. To make his guest feel at ease, he asked her about her work and where she had come from. Encouraged by his interest, the nun told him about their mission with those who were sick in spirit as well as in body. She told him how one of their chapels, dedicated to St Mary Magdalene, was also called the 'Chapel Adventurous' because it was a place of mystery and miraculous visions. She went on to describe how it had a tiny door in its south-facing wall and how, if someone managed to squeeze through this door, their sins would be forgiven.

Deep within himself, Arthur heard a whisper of hope. The holy sister was delighted to hear him promise to visit the nunnery, and, not long after, Arthur made arrangements for the journey. Only his squire was to accompany him, and the two made their way across the inland sea to Beckery. Whilst the mists of Avalon swirled about them, Arthur's unease grew as he felt how close he was to Morgaine's realm, how it drew him, away … and how fragile was the boundary between his world and hers.

When he at last reached Beckery, Arthur would not submit himself to the powers of the chapel's South door straightaway. He wanted time to prepare, time to give himself the best chance of success. He explained to the nuns that during his visit he would like to take the opportunity to go on retreat; accordingly, he fasted and spent the first day in prayer.

That night, he dreamed that he heard a voice summoning him to the Chapel Adventurous – but the following day he dismissed this as being just a dream. On the second night the same thing happened, and again, on waking, Arthur ignored the dream.

On the third night, however, as Arthur's dream was being repeated, his squire was dreaming at the same time that he too heard a voice urging him to go to the chapel. In his dream, the squire obeyed the command, went to the chapel and took one of its candlesticks. Still dreaming, as he was leaving the chapel with it, he was struck down on the threshold by a mighty blow from behind.

The squire, who slept at the foot of the King's bed, woke up screaming – which of course woke the King. He told his master what had happened during his dream, and both marvelled to see the bleeding wound on the back of the squire's head and the actual candlestick. Arthur knew that, ready or not, he had to take the summons of the Chapel Adventurous seriously.

The next night, he went alone to the chapel. There he saw a vision of two hands wielding swords, their blades clashing as they fought up and down the chapel. Beyond them was a monk's body laid out on a bier before the altar. The old priest who was holding mass told Arthur that it was the corpse of one of the holy brothers from Andrewsey. This was one of the blessed pieces of land given to Joseph of Arimathea himself, on which to carry on Christ's work. When the priest continued with the service and reached the part of the mass dedicated to the Eucharist, Arthur saw the Virgin Mary herself. She was carrying the infant Jesus and lifted Him above the altar to offer him up as a sacrifice, and Arthur witnessed the child – rather than the grown man – being slain.

There was Arthur, who had sacrificed his own son only to protect his reputation, and there was Mary, who had sacrificed hers so that Arthur's sins might be forgiven.

At the end of the mass, Mary reached over the bier and gave Arthur a crystal cross. He felt so small and insignificant that it was not difficult for him to crawl out through the South door.

Penitent and hopeful, it is said that King Arthur changed the arms on his shield. Now the background was green for the land he had sworn to protect. It was quartered with a silver cross in gratitude for the one that Mary had given him. In the top right-hand quadrant – the area that shielded his heart in battle – was a depiction of the Virgin and Child.

In the fullness of time, it was little consolation for Arthur to discover that his son, Mordred, had survived – the only baby in the boat who hadn't perished. Mordred would one day rise up against his father, defeat his forces in battle, and at the last inflict on Arthur a mortal wound. If it is true that Morgaine sought revenge, she wrought it through the son of the son of Merlin's man.

⁓ THE DEATH OF ARTHUR ⁓

As Arthur lay dying, he feared that his magical sword Excalibur would fall into the wrong hands. He thought only of finding a way to return it to the Lady of the Lake, who had long ago given it to him, with all its protective powers.

He told one of his most faithful knights, Sir Bedivere, to take the sword and throw it into the nearby River Brue, which flowed through the sacred lake that encircled the Isle of Avalon.

Waiting for Sir Bedivere's return, Arthur knew that the barge of the Priestesses of Avalon had already set out towards him across the misty waters. This boat moved silently, without oars, and could only be commanded by the will of the Priestesses. It was they who controlled the comings and goings between this world and the next.

Sir Bedivere wearily stumbled through the swirling mist towards Pomparles Bridge, which spans the River Brue. He stood on the bridge and raised his arm to throw Excalibur into the seething waters – but the movement never came. He just could not bring himself to fling the precious thing away … what a wasteful act it would be. Instead, he hid it in the rotten heart of a hollow willow, meaning to go back for it later …

When he returned to his dying king, Arthur managed to say, 'Did you do the deed?'

'Yes, my King,' replied Sir Bedivere.

'And what did you see?'

'Nothing, Arthur, just mist and water …'

'You are lying to me! You have not done as you were asked! I thought to have at least one loyal companion at my end. Go back and throw Excalibur into the river, before it is too late …'

Sir Bedivere, ashamed, returned to the hollow willow and retrieved the sword. He went back to the bridge and raised his arm again, held it aloft until it trembled, lowered it. Great were the deeds that Arthur had accomplished with this weapon in his grasp. But now Arthur was dying and could do no more. Yet Sir Bedivere had survived this battle, he still had friends, and there were still many loyal to Arthur's cause. What might he himself not achieve with Excalibur to wield? There was no one to see, no one to know, no one to tell … he could say that Arthur had given Excalibur to him … and so his thoughts ran on as he hid the sword in the tree once more.

'Is the deed done?'

'It is, my King.'

'Tell me what you saw.'

'I saw mist and water and gathering dark …'

'And still you lie to me! Deep will that darkness be if there is not one honest man left in my kingdom. Has it come to this, that there is no one in my darkest hour that I can trust? Go and do as I ask; there will be no more time …'

Such was the anguish in that voice, that Sir Bedivere hastened towards the bridge again. Arthur's body now felt so cold that the damp and clinging mists of Avalon were like the soft warmth of feathers. Already, glimpses of the Other World were brushing past him. He could see the Priestesses' boat drawing nearer, a darker wing on dark water. He could see who was guiding it, seated in its prow.

Sir Bedivere seized the sword for the last time. He rushed onto the bridge and, without taking aim, faster than thought, he flung it as hard as he could. He watched as it soared into the sky, far higher than his spent strength could have sent it. It tore through the heavy clouds and there, where it had wounded the darkness, a beam of light held it in a bright stillness. Brighter and brighter grew that light until Sir Bedivere had to turn his gaze away from that crystal cross with its streaming star-like rays of light.

Slowly as a drifting feather, the sword began to fall – not straight as an arrow but spinning over and over like a leaf in autumn. Down it floated towards the river and, before it could touch the water, a woman's arm clothed in a sleeve of shining white reached up and caught the hilt. For a moment she held it high, then gradually she began to sink. First her arm, then her fist around the pommel and lastly the blade disappeared; and the Lady of the Lake and Excalibur were not seen again.

Sir Bedivere made his way back to the King. He held him in his arms and told him about the arm that had caught the sword.

'You asked me what happened and I have told you. This is what I also saw: I saw light rending the dark, I saw a sacred sign shining above the Sacred Land, I saw Excalibur kept safe from our enemies until the time comes when light springs anew from its blade.'

Arthur smiled at his friend, and whilst he was squeezing his hand he slipped away. His sister Morgaine was there, waiting …

Hundreds of years later, after Glastonbury Abbey had been destroyed by fire, some monks experienced visions of King Arthur. The reigning monarch, King Henry II, was consulted and revealed a royal secret: King Arthur had been buried in the abbey and the knowledge of his exact whereabouts had been passed down through the royal families of Britain. The monks then sought and found a grave, which contained two coffins, with two skeletons: one of a giant of a man, and one of a woman with a plait of yellow hair. Both coffins bore inscriptions declaring the identities of their occupants – Arthur and Guinevere.

Many believe this discovery to have been a medieval fraud, perpetrated to bring more pilgrims and their revenue to alleviate the abbey's temporary financial crisis. But although the coffins and remains have been lost, the drawings and copies of the inscriptions (left by those who once claimed to have seen the originals) tell a different story. Those records show a very early form of writing that medieval monks would have had no knowledge of, and therefore could not have forged.

~ THE ONCE AND FUTURE KING ~

The vast hill at South Cadbury, crowned by some of this country's most extensive earthworks and the site of a mighty battle, is a favoured contender to be identified as Arthur's stronghold, Camelot. Nearby place names bear this out, as in the village of Queen Camel and the nearby River Camel; for all the local people over the centuries, the acceptance of Cadbury as Arthur's court was as evident as the fact that water is wet.

Inside the hill, Arthur lies sleeping with his hundred knights until the time when Britain faces her greatest peril. It is then that the King will awake and gather his knights to defend his country once more.

To keep in practice, every seven years on Midsummer's Eve, or if a Midsummer's Eve falls on a full moon, the gates into the hill are opened, and the King and his retinue ride out. With blazing spears and their mounts shod with silver, they ride along King Arthur's Hunting Causeway towards Glastonbury Tor. A silver horseshoe was found on this track.

In the flank of Cadbury Hill is King Arthur's Well. If you wash your face in its water on Midsummer's Eve, your dreams that night will show you where the gates are hidden, and will take you beyond them to see the sleeping Arthur and his knights.

The hills and moors of Exmoor, with their rugged and unspoiled beauty, remain a wild and haunting place. To this day, their changeable aspect of sweeping skies and plummeting cliffs can veer from the majestic to the foreboding in moments. The particular wildness of its landscape has no doubt contributed to the notoriety of some of its inhabitants, as Exmoor boasts a disproportionately high proportion of highwaymen, murderers, troublesome ghosts and sorcery.

Its moors and combes became, and some would say remain, the last bastion of the pixies. This race could sometimes be helpful, but more often than not would take vengeful offence or play cruel tricks just because they were able to.

‒ The Origin of the Pixies ‒

Long, long ago, when the Devil was still marshalling his forces, he was training his imps in Hell. They were so stubborn and mischievous that at times they challenged even his stamina and deviousness. Whenever he had business on Earth, he couldn't trust them to keep out of trouble, and so he locked them up in cages to cramp their style.

However, these imps had a curious skill with metal, and if they were left unsupervised for any length of time, they would somehow manage to snap the bars of their cages or melt the locks and escape. On one occasion, when the Devil knew that he would have to be away from home longer than usual, he set a watchman to make sure that they stayed locked up.

This poor fool of a man was so gormless and innocent that he should hardly have been in Hell at all. He was too lacking in wits to be considered really wicked, but during his lifetime he had never gone to church and never read his Bible, even though he had owned one and could just about read. Moreover, his devout mother had always begged him to go to services, and she had made sure that he never left the house without a copy of the Holy Book in his jacket pocket. Jan had never resented carrying the extra weight, as it served to squash flies, prop up wobbly tables, or act as a board to cut his hunks of bread and cheese on.

When Jan's earthly time was over, this lack of both observance and respect had sufficed, after long deliberations between the Celestial Committee and the one representative of the Other Place, for Jan to be sent there. And here he now sat, watching the imps watching him.

Whether it was because he could not bear the fierce gaze of their little red eyes, or whether he was just plain bored, he sought something else to look at. It was then that he discovered the Bible which was still in his pocket. No doubt its coating of long-dead flies and mouldy cheese crumbs had allowed it through the Devil's security scanners.

Never in his life had Jan willingly opened his Bible, but now in death he did so. At least it took his mind off those unwavering stares that seemed to pierce him full of burning red holes. Not having done any reading for as long as he could remember, Jan read aloud like a young child. The book was surprisingly interesting, and in any case there was nothing better to do. Jan read on, becoming ever more fluent, like a hinge newly oiled after long disuse.

So absorbed was he that he didn't notice that all the imps had sprung their locks and crept out of their cages. Far from wreaking havoc throughout the Devil's realm, they inched silently closer to Jan. Nobody had ever read them stories before.

When eventually the Devil returned, he too was transfixed – but in his case it was with horror at hearing the words of the Holy Book being spoken aloud in his own front room. Just as dreadful was the sight of all his apprentice imps twisting their scabby little tails with anxiety as Herod gave the order for the massacre of the newly born, and wringing their sooty little hands in anguish as the cock crowed thrice.

At last, the Devil tore himself free from the stories' spell and produced a great flash of flame to attract everybody's attention.

'You've ruined my imps for evermore now that they have heard the words of that cursed Book! They'll be no use to me or any living soul from now until the crack of doom, and neither will you, Jan, with no more wits about you than a crumb of cheese. Be gone from this place and let neither you nor your kind ever come here again!'

There was another flash, and all the imps and Jan found themselves on the Earth, rather than under it. Jan sat blinking on the green grass in the daylight. He had been turned away from both Heaven and Hell, and that is why you will find him wandering the Earth to this day. Almost anywhere that people gather, they will never be more than a few feet away from a man who is equally happy to use his Bible as a doorstop and a book of thrilling stories … it might just be Jan.

Meanwhile, all the imps ran here and there trying to find somewhere less bright and more comfortable. They took to the caves and the darkest, most hidden, valleys and became the pixie folk. The Devil punished them for their lock-picking skills by causing them to be burned by the touch of iron. Since then, they and their kind cannot bear to be near it. Never quite bad enough to be truly wicked, and never quite good enough to be blessed by saint or angel, they remain ever sensitive to insult or rejection, imagined or otherwise.

> We were not good enough for Heaven
> Nor bad enough for Hell
> And therefore unto us 'twas giv'n
> Unseen on Earth to dwell.

Five

ROOT AND BRANCH
What the Trees Know

It is said that there was a time on this island when the forest was so vast that a squirrel could cross from the east to the west coast without once having to touch the ground. If so, that could only have been in the distant days when our ancestors were still hunter-gatherers.

When they started to herd animals and develop agriculture, the felling of the great forests began. The population grew, thereby increasing the need for more crops and domestic animals. People were by now dependent on agriculture, and the forest clearances increased to make space for fields and pastures.

With the discovery of the smiths' craft came the need for the intense temperatures that would smelt metal from rock. This heat could only be achieved by burning hardwood charcoal. With the advent of the Iron Age, even hotter fires were needed to command this harder metal – and they required even more wood for burning.

But in a forested and still pagan world, trees were venerated. Different species were believed, rather like individual people, to have their own qualities and characteristics:

Oh Ellum do grieve and Oak he do hate,
But Willow, Willow, Willow,
Willow do walk if you travel late

It is a curious coincidence that the willow does 'walk', in that it propagates itself by means of detached pieces as small as twigs. These float downstream, or are blown by the wind, and grow wherever they come to rest, be it riverbank or field. All along the same river, the willows would show the same DNA if tested – it is as though the one tree has 'walked' downstream.

Particular trees were imbued with what we would call magical powers; perhaps the distinction between the 'magical' and the 'physical' was not quite as clear-cut then as it is for most of us today. The early British and Celtic tribes revered the 'in between' spaces and times: the twilight; the margin of land revealed at low tide; the skin of the surface of water; the space between the bark and the pith of a tree. The destruction of a tree was not to be undertaken lightly – it could be a chancy thing, and perhaps some latent fear at their wholesale destruction informs the stories we remember to this day.

~ THE ELDER TREE WITCH ~

There was once a farmer and his family who lived in a part of the county near Knighton. As the water could run brackish and the winds blow harsh, there were no large trees on their land and the animals made do with thick hedges for shelter.

This was a part of the county where elder trees were feared – and with good reason. People believed that these trees could be possessed by witches, and that witches could turn themselves into elder trees.

If any doubted, it had happened in living memory – when someone who should have known better took an axe to a taller tree in his hedge to level it off. Perhaps he didn't notice it was an elder, or perhaps he didn't remember the danger when he should have. At the first blow of his axe, the tree began to bleed. Then it screamed and chased him. He only lived to tell the tale because there had been heavy rains and a stream had formed close enough for him to cross its running water. The witch, of course, couldn't follow him over. So that served as a reminder to those who needed it.

A farmer who lived near Knighton made sure that there were no elder saplings in his hedge because he knew the risk. One day, when he went to milk his cows in the far pasture, they didn't yield a drop. He watched them for a day or so to see if they were sickening, but they were grazing well and as contented as ever. The next day, again there was no milk. He thought someone must be stealing it.

That night, he crept into the far pasture to see if he could lay his hands on the thief. It was the dark of the moon and silent. He saw and heard no one, only the steady chewing of the cows and the brushing of grass as they moved through the meadow. There were so many stars winking in the wide, clear sky that he could see the shape of an owl against them. He followed its flight and, as he turned his head, he saw – stark and straight, rising above the hedge – the silhouette of an elder tree.

He fought down his panic and drove the cows to the field nearest his house, not daring to look behind him. When the cattle were all settled, he went to fasten the gate. To his annoyance, the iron chain was missing and he had to roll a boulder against it to keep it closed.

In the morning, he told his family what had happened. His wife was most concerned that he had failed to secure the entrance to the field with the chain, as cold iron is infallible against magic. She shook her head with foreboding when she heard that he hadn't even taken the precaution of reaching through the gate and scraping the sign of the cross in the mud just inside it.

Just then, their daughter looked through the window and cried out that she could see something nearing their cows. She was so frightened that she started running round the house, securing the shutters. The farmer and his wife caught a glimpse of what she had seen: it was an elder tree approaching the cattle.

As soon as she heard this, the grandmother built up the fire with a faggot of ash wood and placed an iron shovel at the ready.

The farmer told his wife to bring him the silver button that had come off his Sunday coat. Needless to say, she had already sewn it back on, but she didn't think it was the moment to say so. She took scissors to the coat and handed him the silver button, with which he loaded his blunderbuss. She then unbarred the door and opened it just enough for him to put the barrel to the crack and peer above it. The witch tree was now so close in amongst the cows that, to shoot from there, could have meant injuring them rather than her. The farmer resolved to get closer, and told his wife to be ready to open the door to him quickly if he had to flee.

It is only the frightened who are truly brave. The farmer forced himself towards the witch to save his cows, forced himself forward as her twiggy hands clawed at their udders. When he was close enough, he shot at her – but his hands were shaking so much that he missed. It was a small miracle that he didn't wound one of his animals, as he had first feared. As soon as she felt the wind of the silver bullet, the witch turned her attention from the cows to him. She raised her skinny arms in the air and flailed them like storm-tossed branches. Screaming like a splitting trunk, she charged. The farmer screamed too, dropped his gun, turned and ran.

His wife had heard and opened the door just in time. He hurtled through, and the tree witch was so close behind him that the wife slammed it straightaway, trapping her husband's coat-tails in it. His daughter replaced the iron bar, shuddering at the sound of the witch's claws scraping against the wood. But she couldn't pass through, because of the iron. There was the farmer trapped by his coat-tails, his arms whirling uselessly as he tried to free himself, but he was too stout to do so, despite the seams beginning to give way.

Now they could hear the witch hurling herself at every door and window of the farmhouse, screaming and scrabbling with rage as she found each one iron-barred against her. It was only a matter of time before she turned to what she could destroy – the pigs or the pony would be next. The farmer was screaming like a stuck pig himself, with the frustration of not being able to get to his pony. If he managed to reach its stall before the witch, he could seize the pony's bridle and throw it over her. This would force her to regain her human form and he would have power over her whilst the bridle held. At last his coat-tails gave way and he flew forward down the passage, skidding along on his belly.

The grandmother stepped over him, holding the iron shovel full of ash embers. She told her granddaughter to open the door. Though she was shaking with fear, one look at her granny was enough for her to know whom she should fear more. She opened the door and retreated. The old woman stood on her threshold and waited as the witch came rushing towards her. Still the old woman stood and waited, waited for her to come even closer, waited for her to come close enough for her aim to be straight and true. Then she flung the shovel full of ashes and the elder tree witch burst into flame.

The grandmother slammed the door shut, but not before all those inside had seen the flames turn blue and heard the angry hiss of boiling sap.

Shortly after, the old woman opened the door to find a huge heap of ash, which was already quite cold. She took the ash-wood cattle goad and drew the sign of the cross on the top of the heap.

Next day, the neighbourhood was buzzing with the story. Many hoped that it was the end of certain individuals whom they suspected of being witches. But Lady —, whose relatives still live in the area, had just been seen hale and hearty in her carriage drawn by a golden pig; and the old sorceress who lived in Steart, whom nobody dared name, was still alive and kicking. It was only when they dared to call upon Raggy Liddy that they found her terribly burned and quite dead, having fallen in her fire.

> Lady, lady all in black
> Silver buttons all down her back
> Alligoshee, alligoshee
> Turnabout all the company
> Lady, lady dressed in black
> Silver buttons all down her back
> Alligoshee, under the tree
> Turn the bridle over me.

Willow is an important crop in Somerset, the Levels offering an ideal habitat for the withy beds. In decline until recently, the industry is slowly being revived: willow sculptures adorn many a local garden; a 'living cathedral' has recently been planted in a Taunton park; and, in these days of conscious sustainability, people are choosing coffins made of woven withies rather than hardwoods.

– Why the Willow Has a Hollow Heart –

There is a strong tradition, mentioned elsewhere in this book, that Jesus spent part of his childhood in Somerset. One day, he asked his mother's permission to go out and play ball, which was given on condition that he behaved himself and didn't get into any mischief.

But who was he to play with? He went off to look for some companions and encountered three other boys. They scorned his invitation, saying that they were high-born, whereas he was merely a poor maid's son who had been born in a stable. This so angered Jesus that he said, 'I may be nothing but a poor maid's son, born in an ox's stall, but I'll have you know at your bitter end, I'm an angel above you all.'

He then ran to the river, which was in flood, and reached his arms up into the air. In his hands he began to catch sunbeams, which his fingers wove into long, gleaming strands of thread. These he plaited into lengths of golden rope. Joining them together, he threw this sunbeam bridge over the churning river. The other boys watched amazed as the sparkling arc held steady across the flood. Then they saw Jesus run across the bridge and wave to them, beckoning from the other bank.

Laughing, they followed him, and when they reached the middle of the bridge, the sunbeams dissolved back into thin air and the boys fell into the river and drowned. Imagine the dismay of Jesus' mother when she saw three weeping women running towards her, begging her to call her son home, as he had drowned theirs. When he returned, she plucked a bunch of withy twigs and with these she gave him a sound whipping, during which Jesus cried out, 'Oh bitter withy! Oh bitter withy, you caused me for to smart. So the willow shall be the very first tree to perish at the heart!'

Since then, willows have always grown hollow as they age, and they are believed to be untrustworthy and unpredictable.

Many kinds of trees are associated with healing powers. Some of their chemical properties are a basis for modern pharmacology: aspirin first being extracted from willow bark, for instance. Other forms of healing took place by 'sympathetic' or symbolic association.

One amusing example describes how someone suffered from piles so badly that not even hospital treatment could help. He was advised by a 'white' witch to carry a conker in his pocket. This fruit of the horse chestnut rather resembles a haemorrhoid, and this was enough to do the trick. Within a few days, the astonished and amused hospital doctor declared that his former patient now looked as though he had never suffered from the condition.

The ancient custom of wassailing the apple trees is strongest in Somerset. The term comes from the Saxon greeting meaning 'good health'. But as apples were also revered by the Celts, it is likely that the ancient custom of blessing or wassailing the orchards predates the later invaders.

Several very ancient wassailing songs survive in this continuing tradition:

Old apple tree, old apple tree,
We be come to worship thee:
To bear and to bow, apples enow
Hatfuls, capfuls, three bushel bags full
Barns full, rabbit holes full
And a little heap under the stairs

During the wassailing ceremony, cider is poured down the trunk of an apple tree. The chosen tree has some apples left on it for the fairy folk, and enough cider should run into the ground for the roots to get the taste of it. Cider-soaked pieces of toast are poked onto the bare twigs and then guns are discharged towards the top of the branches to scare away evil spirits. Although quantities of cider are consumed throughout, underlying the very jolly atmosphere is a respect and gratitude for these providers of plenty.

Another folklore character connected to this time of year is the Apple Tree Man. Seen by only the pure of heart, his face appears in the tree's trunk, but, unlike the ubiquitous Green Man with his mouth stuffed full of leaves, the Apple Tree Man has the gift of speech.

Christmas falls just before the wassailing of the apple trees, and it was even closer before the Gregorian calendar was adopted. A strongly held belief in Somerset was that the animals which were in the stable when Jesus was born are, as the clocks strike midnight on Christmas Eve, gifted with human speech.

The apple tree stood in the garden
Its blossoms as white as the snow, the snow

And there in the cool of the evening
Our dear Lord God He did go, He did go.
But Old Mother Eve she liked apples
And Adam he liked them too, liked them too
The Serpent he hid in the garden
A-twined about the tree, the tree
'You never did eat of such wonderful meat
And so honey sweet,' said he, said he.
But Old Mother Eve she liked apples
And Adam he liked them too, liked them too
They turned them both out of the garden
Shut out with a fiery key, key, key
But Old Man Adam he rolled up his sleeves
And planted an apple tree, tree, tree.
But Old Mother Eve she liked apples
And Adam he liked them too, liked them too
There are apple trees down in the garden
There are orchards in valleys below
In autumn and spring the apple is king
And we bless it wherever we go.

∽ THE APPLE TREE MAN ∽

There was once an old widower farmer who was a bitter and penny-pinching man. Some said that his bitterness was on account of losing his young wife, and that his penny-pinching was on account of him having to feed and clothe the two little boys she had left him with.

Others said that his miserly ways were due to his disappointment at not finding the Dane Hoard. This was the treasure that legend told was buried on the farm, or thereabouts. The farmer had neglected his work and neglected his sons, spending every spare moment digging for it. Much of his land was pitted like the old lead mine hollows up on the Mendips, but he had never found the treasure – if indeed it was ever there to be found.

As for his sons, the elder was as mean and bitter as his father, but the younger was as open-hearted and generous as a summer's day.

'Must of took after his mother,' said the villagers.

No one was surprised when the widower died on a grim February day and left everything to his elder son. Like father, like son in this case; as soon as the will had been read, the elder brother said, 'Well, Jan, now that this is all mine, I want you out by sunset tomorrow.'

'But where shall I go?' asked his poor brother.

'There's the old shack in the bottom paddock with that old donkey and ox, so far gone not even the knacker would take them. But I'll want rent, mind. A silver piece to be paid on Christmas Day or you're out.'

So the younger brother moved into the paddock in the bitter weather, into a shack that was so tumbledown he wouldn't have put a dog in it. But what was worse was the sight of those poor animals, too weak from starvation to break through the neglected hedges and forage elsewhere.

The first thing he did was to beg some hay from a neighbour to feed them. Then he brushed away the snow from some healing plants and mixed them with a mash made with elder bark, to treat their coughs. He begged some honey from another neighbour to put on their sores, and only when all this had been done did he see what he could make of the old shack.

There he found the remains of a few abandoned tools, some with blades but no handles and some with handles but no blades. Nevertheless, they were better than nothing and he patched and mended and made do. As night fell on that short and bitter day, he fed and dosed the animals again, and now they had just enough strength to lift their heads a little and nuzzle his hand.

It wasn't long before word got around about how badly he had been treated, and he was always the first to be offered work if there was any going – which was seldom enough. From time to time he would find that something useful had been left for him by the paddock gate – perhaps an old blanket, a few logs or half a sack of last season's apples.

So it was that Jan managed; with his care, all around him in that place began to thrive. Before the month was out he had pruned all the old fruit trees, so neglected that they hadn't fruited for years. He used the manure from the ox and donkey for fertiliser, and he wove and cut back what he could rescue of the hedges, and even laid some more. He broke up a stretch of ground, kneeling to do it as the mattock had no handle, but at last it was dug and weeded for planting vegetables.

However hard he worked for nearby farms, he and the animals ate up all his wages. And now there were more to feed, as those that his brother mistreated found their home with him. There were a few ducks and chickens, a one-eyed cat and an old lurcher. Starting with next to nothing, there was so much he needed all at once that every penny he earned was immediately spent. He wondered how he would pay his rent.

Now it was spring, and the trees he had tended blossomed. He had made withy hurdles to keep the animals from his vegetable bed and these were sprouting nicely. Tibby the cat was an excellent mouser in spite of her one eye, and she kept the vermin out of the animal feed. The ox was now so well recovered that Jan hired him out to plough a neighbour's land in exchange for a share of the crops to come. The rabbits were breeding and the lurcher brought back plenty to share. The poultry were laying well.

The donkey too had regained his strength and was loaned out in exchange for some old planks and some nails. With these, Jan made a stable for him and the ox. He loaned the donkey again in exchange for a supply of straw, and all of the animals moved in together. There was enough for everyone, but never a spare penny to save.

Spring gave way to summer and Jan used the longer hours of daylight to work harder. There were so many clutches that he was selling chicks and ducklings as well as eggs. Those earnings went on a pair of boots and making his old shack weatherproof – the first money he had spent on himself apart from food. The fruit had set on the trees, the hedges would be full of nuts and berries, and the chickens were keeping the root crops free from pests. They would get through the approaching cold weather more easily than last time, if only he could find the rent.

Since that cold February day, Jan had not spoken to his brother, who had shown no interest in how he was managing. But the elder son had his own concerns. Like father, like son – his whole life had now become a treasure hunt. He neglected the farm and dug where there was no sign of the earth having been disturbed before, still without finding any sign of treasure. People in the village said that he would go mad with it. Some said he already had – to treat his poor brother so.

Autumn slipped into winter, and Jan gathered the little crop of cider apples when the first frosts had had a good chance to nibble at them. Another friendly farmer allowed him to use his cider press, and though the cider barely filled an old keg rather than a barrel, it was more than anyone could have expected those neglected trees to produce. Now that it was December, Jan was looking with regretful eyes at all he had created, because he knew that, without the rent, his brother wouldn't hesitate to turn him out in the snow.

He reached for the little keg to cheer himself with the glow of cider, and found that much of it had seeped away through a crack he hadn't noticed. Jan felt that his luck had run out with the drink. But when you have been down so low that you can't go down any further, there is only one way to go after that.

Jan remembered the time of year and that he had yet to attend a wassail. He thought of how he might never tend his little orchard again, and went to the oldest of the trees that he had rescued, carrying the last of the cider. Tibby followed him, twining between his ankles and the base of the tree, whilst he pulled a crust of bread from his pocket and poked it onto some bare twigs.

Then he tipped the firkin over the base of the branches, splashed the last few drops at the foot of the trunk, and sang:

Old Apple Tree we wassail thee
And hoping thou wilt bear
For the Lord doth know where we shall be
Till apples come next year.
For to bear well, and to bear well
So merry let us be
Let every man take off his hat
And shout to the Old Apple Tree!
Old Apple Tree, we wassail thee
And hoping thou wilt bear
Hatfuls, capfuls and three bushel bagfuls
And little heaps under the stairs
Hip, Hip, Hooray!

His voice rang through the frosty air, but he felt so lonely singing all by himself that he didn't have the heart to cheer three times.

'Now run along little Tibby back to the stable and don't be meddling with things that don't concern you,' came a deep voice.

Jan was sure that there was no one else in the orchard, but he looked around as the cat ran off. There were only the silent criss-cross shadows caught between starlight and snowlight. Then, in the stillness, the tree's branches rustled, and where they joined the trunk there was a shimmering. The rough gnarling of the bark was now a mouth and the knotholes had become eyes, wrinkling like old pippins as the Apple Tree Man smiled.

'We have been watching you now for the best part of the year, boy, when we thought your sort had forgotten us. I don't need to tell you this – but for your kindness to us, and the other creatures that live in this orchard, I will. That scoundrel brother of yours has been wasting his life like your father before him, digging for that Dane Hoard. But like his father he'll never find it – because only you and I know that the treasure is buried right here where you're standing.'

All that remained of the Apple Tree Man was one knot-hole eye, which winked at him before it disappeared. The next day would be Christmas Eve. Jan rushed to get his tools and desperately attacked the frozen ground beneath the set of footprints nearest the tree. At last his pick clawed through the topsoil to a layer that hadn't been reached by the frost. He dug with his broken spade and felt something solid; then came the rasp of metal on metal. Soon the old iron box was in his hands, so rusted through that the gleams between his fingers looked like handfuls of starlight.

Jan hid the treasure in his old boots, which he hadn't thrown away as Tibby liked to curl up in them – but tonight she would find herself a softer bed in the stable. Then he returned to the orchard, and, as best he could, hid the signs of his digging. That night there was a heavy snowfall and no trace of his efforts remained.

The next day he had a visitor. This was the first time his brother had sought him out, and it was only to remind him that his rent was due the next day.

'Where did you get they?' he asked suspiciously, pointing at the ox and the donkey. They were now in such good condition that he didn't recognise them. 'Well, 'tis certain you'll be paying your rent tomorrow if you could pay the price of they beasts,' he sneered.

Seeing the animals had reminded the older brother of the old story about the beasts that were present in the stable when Jesus had been born. Tradition told that on Christmas Eve, during the twelve strokes of midnight, they were given the gift of human speech, and had the power to grant wishes. Perhaps he could ask them where the treasure was hidden. It was worth a try, and he decided to return secretly later.

Just before midnight, he crept back to the orchard and slipped into the stable. There wasn't long to wait before he heard the village clock strike, and straightaway he heard the animals begin to speak.

'Are you awake, Brother?' asked the donkey.

'I be now,' came the ox's reply.

'Remember that miserable boy up at the farm who treats his own brother as badly as he treated us beasts?'

'Well, what mortal could forget him?'

'For all as how he's mistreated us he's still crept in here so brazen as a Beauty of Bath to ask us a favour.'

'What would that be now, and him so bold as bucking bullock?'

'He wants to know where that gurt treasure, the Dane Hoard, be buried.'

'He do, do he?'

'But he won't never know, on account of it being buried no more. He's too late, they that is more deserving has found it avore him.'

If hearing human speech coming from an ox and an ass was the strangest thing that the older brother had ever witnessed, then hearing human laughter coming from these animals was especially unpleasant. They turned their huge open mouths with their great yellow teeth towards him, and their sleek barrel-shaped bodies heaved so much that it was a wonder they didn't crack a rib.

When the clock had chimed twelve times, the animals continued their row, only now it was only lowing and braying – though the man knew that they were still laughing at him. Their master turned in his sleep at their racket, and the other man slunk away with his hopes dashed.

He returned later that day, hoping at least to have the satisfaction of throwing his brother out in the snow, but the place was deserted. There, in the patched-up hovel, on an upturned log (which was all there was for a table), gleamed a single silver piece.

Far away on some distant hill, his younger brother was walking with the lurcher at his heels. The old donkey was carrying panniers of ducks and poultry. The ox was ambling ahead of them, with Tibby riding in style. When they passed a stranger on the road, the young man heard his first Christmas greeting.

'Blessings of the season.'

'And a Merry Christmas to you, friend.'

The stranger studied the peculiar band of travellers with a shrewd eye, noticing the old, tightly laced boots hung around the youth's strong shoulders.

'Be you going far?'

'Happen so,' came the reply.

The oak had always been considered the strongest and most valuable of trees, and to fell one was a fearful undertaking. Sometimes, however, it could not be avoided — as in the case of an oak that had become the haunt of a malevolent spirit.

— THE HAUNTED OAK TREE —

Close to the bottomless pit into which the corrupt Judge Popham had been thrown by his horse, there grew a magnificent specimen. Most were glad to be rid of this evil man and believed him to be in the right place, the pit being so deep that people thought it was a direct shortcut to Hell. However, due to the intercession of his wife's frequent prayers, his spirit was not to remain there. She had spent her life trying to reform him, and now his spirit was to be given a chance to do penance.

The Powers That Be permitted Popham's ghost to emerge from the pool and to take one cock's stride per year towards the church. This continued for some years until Popham reached the oak tree, whereupon his spirit moved into the tree and refused to leave. Moreover, it exerted its malevolence over anyone who ventured near that spot, and tried particularly hard to cause riders to be thrown into the bottomless pool to meet a similar end to his own. Every time some malicious act was perpetrated, the tree would creak and groan with protest.

The area was now so dangerous that a 'white' wizard was consulted – and he advised that the oak would have to come down. Few were prepared to risk that undertaking. It was well known that an oak could defend itself, but that if it was overcome, it would scream as it was uprooted and anyone hearing that scream would become mad.

At last, some brave volunteers were found. They stopped up their ears and used a team of horses and thick iron chains. As soon as the horses took a step, the chains burst asunder and everyone was so frightened that they ran away.

Though the chains were mended by three blacksmiths, working together for good luck, it was nearly impossible to find anyone who would make another attempt. Eventually, a devout ploughman said that he would do the job. He borrowed ten oxen, choosing those that he had seen, over the years, kneeling down in the straw at the stroke of midnight on Christmas Eve. Then, Bible in hand, he sang hymns, pausing only to call the oxen. At their first stride the tree came out of the ground as easily as a child picks a daisy, although its scream could be heard miles away, muffled through covered ears. As the great oak fell, Popham's spirit fled into a nearby wood, where it remains to this day – though considerably weakened by being so successfully thwarted.

The oak is a tree associated with a sense of justice; it offers protection for the righteous and is capable of exposing criminals, exacting terrible revenge on those who deserve it.

⁓ THE CRUEL SHIP'S CARPENTER ⁓

A ship's carpenter had got his girlfriend pregnant and wanted to get rid of her before the baby was born. She was heavily pregnant by the time he was due to go on his next voyage, and he thought the timing was just right to do away with her before he left.

He lured Polly to a deserted place, where he murdered her, and he then immediately joined his ship, which set sail down the Bristol Channel towards the Atlantic. However, the oak from which the ship had been built had other ideas – and the ship, having reached the middle of the Channel, refused to move. The vessel resisted wind, sail, oars and tide … and the captain and crew knew that she was 'galleyed' – under the influence of magic. Clearly there was someone on board who shouldn't be, and clearly the ship would go nowhere until that person was found.

After the ship had been searched and no stowaway had been found, every man was made to swear on the Bible that he had done nothing to bring this situation about. When it came to the carpenter's turn, he took the same oath. As he was speaking, Polly's corpse rose out of the water and glided onto the boat. She seized him and – as though he were a piece of sailcloth – tore him into two pieces, throwing his rent body overboard; one half for her life and the other for her baby's.

It was only when rough justice had been done that the ship's oaken timbers allowed the boat to sail on.

⁓ THE SOMERTON MURDER ⁓
AND THE HANGING TREE

There was once a beautiful young woman, one of the travelling people, who every summer camped on the Summer Lands in the Brue Valley. She formed an unfortunate liaison with the local squire, who was married. His wife grew suspicious, and as he feared that she would find out about his lover, he stabbed poor young Sally to death, and hid her body in a huge, hollow oak tree just outside Somerton.

Soon after, a herdsman was driving cattle along the drovers' road by which this tree stood. The cows refused to pass it and preferred to face his whip or dogs rather than move on. Realising that something uncanny was going on, the drover looked inside the tree and found the corpse, which he carried to the market square.

Sally's body was placed under the butter cross, and each of the local men was required to approach the corpse in turn. As soon as the squire did so, the many stab wounds began to bleed afresh, and at this sign the squire confessed his crime. He was hanged at the crossroads from the 'Hanging Elm', a tree often used for this purpose.

So many had been hanged from its branches that it became a well-known haunted spot, exerting its influence even after having been ravaged by Dutch elm disease. It grew just outside Somerton, a small country town where King Ine, the first King of Wessex, had established his capital.

Somerton's steep approaches were ideal for highwaymen's purposes, as riders and coaches had to slow down to manage the slopes. Many who had robbed in that vicinity had their corpses left on the tree after the hangings, as a warning to others.

Oh I am a robber, a right roaring blade
And now I'm in jail because of my trade
All because of my trade boys, the judge says to me:
You must swing my fine lad on the High Gallows Tree
Oh fetter my ankles, my hands and my waist,
And give me a nosegay all in finest of taste;

> And dress me in buckskins so handsome and free
> To wear for my dance on the High Gallows Tree

The place where this elm once stood is still unchancy, and many cars have inexplicably lost their power there. Local motor mechanics called out to that spot insist on parking their rescue vehicles well away from it, and pushing the broken-down vehicles up to theirs, as they know that otherwise the cars' electrics will not work properly.

Britain's holiest tree, the Glastonbury Thorn, grew until recently on Wearyall Hill. Never has Glastonbury's community been so united in horror as when, on a morning in the winter of 2010, this precious hawthorn was discovered sawn and mutilated. It was so severely vandalised that it did not survive the attack. Fortunately, its cousin continues to flourish in St John the Baptist's churchyard, and Her Majesty the Queen is reputed to have said that a favourite moment in her year is when one of its flowering branches is brought to her every December.

⁓ THE LEGEND OF THE GLASTONBURY THORN ⁓

Joseph of Arimathea, Jesus' wealthy and respected uncle, used to bring his nephew Jesus to these shores to teach him about tin mining and trading. They would sometimes disembark at Pilton near Glastonbury, in the days when it was still an island amidst an inland sea. The nearby escarpment of Wearyall Hill still clearly shows where the ancient beach stretched along its eastern flank.

But Jesus' path was destined to follow the spiritual rather than the material, and soon his life was focused on the land of his birth. After the crucifixion, his corpse was given into Joseph of Arimathea's care.

At that time, both Jewish and Roman law stated that relatives were responsible for the burial, whatever the cause of death, and that in the case of a criminal it had to take place by nightfall on the same day. His uncle was therefore allowed to take charge of the body, even though he was suspected of sharing Jesus' beliefs and was known to have spoken out against his sentence. In any case, all those associated with Jesus, especially his family, were at great risk of persecution, and so Joseph of Arimathea decided to flee, possibly with other companions who had also been close to Jesus.

Before he set out on his journey, he made a wooden staff. Some say that it was made with the wood from the very cross to which Jesus had been nailed. Others say it was from the thorn tree that had provided the crown of thorns that had played such a memorable part in Jesus' mockery and torment. Joseph is said to have destroyed this tree in the process, so that it could never again provide the means for torturing another unfortunate.

Joseph fled from one edge of the Roman Empire to its furthest extremity. He returned to Somerset where he had powerful friends.

Disembarking near Glastonbury, he began to climb Wearyall Hill. As his staff sank into the damp ground, it immediately began to blossom, and Joseph said, 'This is a good and holy land.'

His staff took root and became the tree known as the Glastonbury Thorn, loved and visited regularly by locals and tourists from all over the world. Apart from the miraculous way in which this tree had instantly rooted and flowered, it had the added peculiarity of blossoming both at Christmas and at Easter. It is referred to in many local songs:

Let us kneel in the hay for 'tis Christmas Day
When the cock sings 'Christ is born'
And there's bloom on the twig, and the little lambs do jig
When the cock sings 'Christ is born'
And the robin sang, oh the little robin sang
So sweetly sanged he
On Christmas morn, on the blessed thorn,
On a twig of the Holy Tree

This particular verse also refers to the tradition that the robin, our beloved winter bird, acquired his red breast when he plucked some of the thorns away from Jesus' crown during the crucifixion. His feathers were stained with blood, and all his descendants still bear the mark of this holy act of compassion.

This double blossoming, at the time of Christianity's most important festivals, was so imbued with significance that cuttings were taken and planted at other sites in Glastonbury and in churchyards around Somerset.

Not so long ago, a sample of the Glastonbury Thorn was taken away for scientific analysis. This was done under protest from some members of the pagan community, who objected to any form of deliberate damage, however small. The ecclesiastic authorities and legend lovers of all persuasions were delighted to learn that the tree's DNA showed that it was a rare species of hawthorn only to be found in a small region

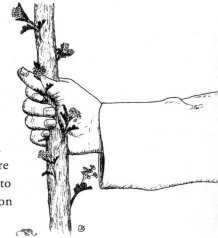

of the Middle East, on the borders between Syria, Israel and Palestine.

An earlier act of destruction was perpetrated by the Puritans centuries ago during the Civil War, as they considered the tree to be an object of idolatry. How they would have disapproved of all the offerings – particularly of the 'clooties', strips of coloured cloth – that festooned the branches of the tree that was planted as soon as Cromwell was deposed! And ever since, the tradition of lovingly decorating the tree has continued.

Throughout the winter of 2010, around the maimed trunk of the desecrated and now branchless tree, a multicoloured shrine was growing. An installation was created that would grace any modern art gallery.

The community watched the trunk anxiously for any sign of recovery in the spring of 2011, and a short-lived hope accompanied the appearance of a few green buds on 17 March, Joseph of Arimathea's saint's day. These opened on the vernal equinox, the first day of spring, 21 March. But these leaves were the last, and the decision has now been made to take out the lifeless stump.

Even in these modern times, the Glastonbury Thorn is so revered that its damaged branches have been saved, awaiting their transformation into sculptures for Glastonbury's various shrines. As these words are being written, the town's diverse communities are planning the ceremonies that will accompany the planting of its replacement.

> Oh Joseph came a-sailing all over the sea
> A-bringing a twig of the Holy thorn tree.
> From the bitter cruel cross of our own sweet Lord
> Oh Joseph, Joseph, Joseph was a tinner was he.

Six

STANDING STONES, RUNNING WATER

Close to what is now Bristol Airport, with its metallic sea of parked cars, there used to be found a most magical place …

~ GOBLIN COMBE ~

Long ago, when we were in touch with powers from beneath the Earth, some children went into Goblin Combe to gather primroses, a favourite flower amongst all the fairy folk. At the end of the day, the youngest child became separated from her companions, and, placing her bunch of primroses upon a great rock, she began to cry.

Now, this rock happened to be an entrance to the Goblin Kingdom beneath, and her tears pattered down upon it. The goblins thought that the little girl had given them a gift of primroses, which were hard for them to gather, as they never emerged from their underworld during daylight. Just as the sun set, the great rock split open and soon the combe was full of the creatures, spilling out into the twilight. Normally the fairy folk show an aversion to salt, but the goblins did not object to the child's salty tears that had fallen onto their threshold, as they could tell that they had been shed by an innocent.

Delighted with their gift, the goblins took the child into their underground kingdom and played with her until not even their wonders could keep her awake any longer. Then they gave her a present of a ball made of the purest gold and set her on her way.

She was met in the combe by an anxious and fearful search party, who had come equipped with lanterns and holy water. All marvelled at the golden ball and at the tale she told.

Soon after, a troupe of travelling players came through the village. They too heard the story, and one of their party, a juggler, decided that he would like a golden ball or two for himself. He asked to be shown the goblins' rock and then went to pick a bunch of primroses. When the villagers saw him heading back down the combe with the flowers, they realised what he was about to do, and warned him earnestly against it. The juggler ignored them, and some followed him hoping to get him to change his mind. They saw him hurry up to the rock and strike it with the primroses. It cracked open and swarming figures dragged the juggler inside. He was never seen again.

✿

The only hot springs in Britain are at Bath. Scrapers found 18ft beneath the abbey show that the springs have been used since the Stone Age. They have been venerated as a holy place and dedicated to a succession of deities throughout history. Bronze Age Celts consecrated the springs to their tribal goddess, Sulis, and regarded the heat of the waters as a manifestation of this solar deity. Her emblem was the hazel tree, and a hazel wand cut at

Midsummer was believed to reveal buried treasure and water, these finds also symbolising wisdom and enlightenment.

The invading Romans, exceptionally, allowed the resident Belgae tribe to continue running this sacred site themselves, as not even the Roman state could have improved on its management. As was their custom throughout the empire, the Romans adopted the local deities, and worship continued at what was now being called Aqua Sulis.

Women, both British and Roman, would throw hazelnuts into the waters hoping for a cure for barrenness; centuries later, huge numbers of these nuts were found when a new pump was installed. This discovery prompted the seventeenth-century anti-quarian Thomas Guidot to pronounce that the nuts were left over from Noah's flood, which God had planned for the autumn: 'Providence by that means securing the revival of the Vegetable World …'

For centuries, these unique springs have been a place of pilgrim-age for health seekers …

Which waters heate and cleansing perfect power,
With vapours of the sulphur, salts and fire,
Hath vertue great, to heale, and washe and scowre
The bathed sores therein that health desire

… the first and most famous being …

~ KING BLADUD ~

Prince Bladud was son and heir to King Lud of the ancient Britons. He studied in Athens and became a very learned man, but as his father was growing old, he returned to Britain accompanied by four Greek philosophers, with whom he hoped to educate the court.

This, however, was not to be, as whilst he was away he had contracted the deforming skin disease, leprosy. In those days leprosy was a scourge, and lepers were excluded from the community to live in seclusion or in their own colonies. Bladud might be heir to the throne, but as a leper he would never be allowed to rule.

He was banished from the court, but, as he was leaving, his mother gave him a ring with which to prove his identity if he should ever need to do so. So it was that Bladud left the palace carrying a staff in one hand and a bell in the other, which had to be rung as a warning to people that a leper was approaching.

His supplies of food soon ran out, and he became destitute. Not knowing how else to survive, he begged a farmer to allow him to be a swineherd and graze his pigs, thinking that no one could object to him having this solitary occupation. The farmer agreed, and Bladud took charge of the herd. Great was his horror after a few weeks to discover that the pigs had developed the same dreadful skin disease as himself. Fearing the farmer's anger, he drove the pigs deep into the most remote part of the forest, hoping to stay hidden with them there.

One day, far from human habitation, the pigs found a wallow where the mud had a very strong and strange smell. Bladud could see its vapours against the dark trunks of the surrounding trees. As he approached he could feel warmth, and realised that what he was seeing was steam. The pigs delighted in this heated mud bath, barely emerging even to feed. As they were in such a secluded place and the warm spring offset the chill of autumn, Bladud didn't move them on.

He could hardly believe it when, after a few days, their skin condition began to improve. It wasn't long before their skin was completely clear, and Bladud decided to see if wallowing in the strange mud would have any effect on him. To his amazement, he too was soon cured.

Losing no time, he drove the pigs back to the farmer before making his way to his parents' court. There he entrusted his mother's ring to a servant, and asked him to place it in the Queen's drinking vessel. When the Queen found it, she declared that it was the very same that she had given her son – and demanded to know how it had reached her cup. Prince Bladud was led into the hall, looking like a beggar. When his rags, matted hair and beard had all been cut away, the King and Queen recognised their son, and everyone could see that his skin was free from disease.

When in due time he inherited the throne, Bladud set about building a city around the healing springs, so that people could be cured of many ailments. He also rewarded the pig farmer who had been so kind to him, by giving him a large piece of land that included his nearest village.

This glorious prince of royal race,
The founder of this happy place,
Where Beauty holds her reign,
To Bladud's memory let us join,
And crown the glass from Springs Divine
His Glory to maintain
Though long his languish did endure,
The bath did lasting health procure,
And Fate no more did frown,
For smiling Heaven did invite,
Great Bladud to enjoy his right,
And wear the imperial crown

'Good' King Bladud came to a curious end. Having continued his studies throughout his city-building period – which included setting up a university in Lincolnshire – he taught himself to fly, albeit with the help of artificial wings. These he decided to try out in London, and there are two different eyewitness accounts as to what happened next. All say that he was clearly seen to take off from the White Tower and fly high into the sky.

Some say that he soared above the crowd and then disappeared as an angel into the next world. Others say that he flew only for a short time and then fell to his death, breaking his neck on the roof of the Temple of Apollo.

> May all a fond ambition shun,
> By which e'en Bladud was undone,
> As ancient stories tell,
> Who try with artful wings to fly,
> But towering on the regions high,
> He down expiring fell

Perhaps the reader may think that this second version of events is the more plausible. However, as Bladud is thought to have been born between 910 and 836 BC, almost 1,000 years before the Roman Conquest, he must also have been a Time Lord to have crashed into a Roman temple!

An alternative version of the story shows a 'Bad' King Bladud in quite a different light. No pitiful story of exile and joyful redemption does he present, but tales of the dark arts. His consort was the pagan goddess of the springs, and to please her he kept the waters hot by means of magical fires. These were kept alight by a constant supply of human sacrifices; when the waters cooled, no ashes could be seen but only hard, rounded stones.

This darker story of the same personage harks back to Druid sacrifices, so well documented by the Romans. The stones may well be one of the earliest references to coal being used in this country, as coal was mined close to Bath centuries later.

The Mendip Hills are full of caves, gorges and strange rock forma-tions. One of these, in Burrington Combe, has a fissure all down its length. This rock gave protection to a grateful sightseer during a violent storm, and so was immortalised in the famous hymn 'Rock of Ages'. Excavations have revealed prehistoric animal and human remains, including Cheddar Man: at 9,000 years, he is the world's oldest complete skeleton. When a DNA testing programme was carried out in the area to see whether he had any living relatives, his closest relation proved to be the local headmaster!

Some of the human finds are amongst our most gruesome. Whether the cannibalism revealed by forensic science was born of hunger, or due to ritualistic practices, is still being discussed – par-ticularly in the case of the oldest drinking vessels made of human skulls to be found in the world.

It was the practice of our ancestors to bury their dead in caves, and there were many such ritual burials in the cave systems beneath the Mendips. A ritual burial of skeletons placed in a circle was found in Aveline's Hole, a cave in Burrington Combe, now known to be the oldest cemetery in Britain.

Through the cave known as Wookey Hole runs the River Axe, which rises very rapidly, depending on rainfall. Consequently, debris used to be washed from the cave into the village of Wookey. Some of this debris consisted of human bones, and may have given rise to the tale of …

— THE WITCH OF WOOKEY HOLE —

There was once a witch who lived in a cave called Wookey Hole, just above the village of that name. As a young woman she had been crossed in love, and the bitterness that then consumed her had turned her towards the dark arts.

Having taken up residence in the cave, she devoted the rest of her life to acts of wickedness, each more evil than the last. The witch had a particular hatred for young lovers and would cast spells that lured them to her lair, where they would be murdered and eaten. And didn't the human bones that appeared from time to time in the water that ran through the village prove this?

In time, her infamy reached the ears of the Bishop of Wells and he dispatched one of his own to get rid of her. This was a monk whose fiancée had died when he was a young man. Despairing of life, he had renounced the world, finding comfort only in holy words and deeds.

Equipped with a crucifix and holy water blessed by the bishop, he entered the cave holding the cross before him. At this sight, the witch fled further into the cave – not out of fear, but as a ploy to entice him deeper into her stronghold. The monk followed her until she could run no further, when she turned on him, screaming curses that blasted great chunks out of the rock face. With no time even to unstopper the bottle of holy water, he flung it at her. It hit a rock and shattered, sprinkling her with the contents and instantly turning her to stone.

If you are brave enough to visit the cave today, you can see her stalagmite, a hideous old woman wearing a bonnet, perfectly 'captured' in stone. Her cat familiar, also turned to stone, remains in the cave, but the witch's crystal ball was retrieved in case it fell into the wrong hands, and can now be viewed in the local museum.

If you were to take the road along what is called the 'Hog's Back', a ridge that stretches from Butleigh to Bridgewater, you would pass a sign — barely visible amongst the trees — pointing to Swayne's Leaps. Also referred to as Swayne's Jumps, their story recalls the pitiful events of the Monmouth rebellion.

Although the terrible events of the Civil War must still have been fresh in people's minds, there were nevertheless those who were prepared to risk all to challenge the succession to the throne. The Duke of Monmouth's forces advanced through Somerset and he was finally defeated at the Battle of Sedgemoor, where there is a stone memorial to his ill-fated enterprise.

On the night before his final defeat he met with Mother Shipton, a prophetess who had moved to Somerset and whose reputation had preceded her. Fortunately, not all of her prophesies came to pass and Ham Hill was not submerged by a flood, despite the local inhabitants evacuating just in case! However, on this occasion, Monmouth would have done well to pay her more heed, as she exhorted him to: 'Beware the rhine, beware the rhine!'

He thought the old woman must be wandering in her wits to be referring to a major river in Germany, but of course she was speaking about a particular feature of the landscape — the rhines — drainage ditches that cross the Somerset Levels. In the course of that night, Monmouth's cavalry was trapped in a rhine with particularly deep waters and steep banks, where they became sitting targets for the government infantry encamped on the other side.

The ensuing battle was more of a rout; Monmouth's forces were defeated and the round up of those loyal to him began. There are countless testimonies of the terrible revenge that was perpetrated on these unfortunates — in particular by the infamous Judge Jeffries,

who is still so hated in these parts that people of the same name are
refused rooms at local inns. In this time of bloody turmoil, brother
was set against brother, father against son and whole villages were
divided.

～ THE LEAPING STONES ～

It didn't take long for government forces to be informed
about one Jan Swayne, an impoverished farm worker with
a large family who lived on a piece of undrained marsh near
Sedgemoor. He was arrested, his hands were tied behind his
back, and he was marched off under armed guard to a place of
public execution.

One of the guards, John Marsh, had been his friend all
their lives. As they marched near Whitley Wood on the Hog's
Back, he asked his captain whether they shouldn't have some
sport before the prisoner died. Marsh went on to explain that
Swayne was the best sportsman in the region and could out-
wrestle or outrun any man, and the captain agreed that Swayne
would be allowed to show what he could do as long as his
hands remained tied behind him.

The soldiers stood back to watch as Swayne said that he
would show them his skill at the long jump. He leaped in an
unexpected direction, towards the edge of the steep escarpment. So enormous was this jump, at 22ft, that the soldiers
just watched in astonishment. The next leap was made from a
standstill and measured 20ft, and the third was 18ft, amongst
the trees, and over the edge, running like a deer to disappear
with his hands still tied.

Jan Swayne got clean away. He is remembered as a hero,
and as an emblem for all those who weren't so lucky. Three

stone slabs were set in the ground to mark the location of these prodigious leaps. They can still be seen to this day, silent testimonies to defiance and friendship.

~ STONES PLACED TO PLEASE ~

There are three roads entering Glastonbury, two of which are accessed via large roundabouts. Some years ago, the local council decided to make the most of these spaces and lovingly planted shrubs and flowers on them. These were further graced by enormous, roughly hewn, honey-coloured stone edifices placed in their midst.

If there had been a national roundabout competition, these would definitely have won on aesthetic grounds – but there is no pleasing some people. The following day, the council switchboard was besieged by irate local Christians, furious with the erection of 'pagan standing stones'. The day after, the council switchboard was again besieged, this time by local Druids and pagans all objecting because the 'standing stones' had been incorrectly placed: they had not been laid out along any of the available ley lines!

Who knows what superhuman efforts were subsequently made to please everyone at the next roundabout enhancement exercise … whatever they were, they were successful – and it may be the only occasion in the entire history of public art when there have been no complaints.

This roundabout, once dull and unadorned, lies outside Shepton Mallet, a town whose name suggests a long association with all that sheep have meant to the area. A sculptor was therefore commissioned to carve a flock of stone sheep. When these were unveiled, they were all seen to be safely grazing in their appointed places.

The embellishment, however, proved to be only too successful, putting the passing motorists in danger. So appealing were these sheep that the drivers negotiating the roundabout were gazing at them grazing – and were paying, therefore, scant attention to the road. Furthermore, the local populace took them to their hearts, and they became the focus of a guerrilla community arts movement.

At every festival – Christian or pagan – secret teams, under cover of darkness, would clothe the sheep in whatever costumes suited the season. They have been dressed up as Father Christmas and his elves, worn garlands of flowers at Midsummer and been equipped with bats' wings, masks and brooms at Halloween. Their Easter bonnets would have drawn looks of envy from the Ladies' Enclosure at Ascot, and on one May Day the council had to step in again – this time to limit the creative urge.

As dawn broke on that May morning, the flock was found dancing around its own maypole. Each ewe was attached to her own brightly coloured ribbon and was wearing a crown of May blossom. Other streamers fluttered loose in the breeze, as an invitation to those not yet part of the flock to join the happy throng. Sadly but wisely the maypole was removed, as it was such a distraction to drivers.

Even so, motorists are still to be seen pulling up on the roundabout in broad daylight to adjust some garment that the elements have displaced.

Unlike the stones in the previous story, many achieve fame by moving around in an unexpectedly animated manner, often going to particular pools or rivers to drink. Some stand sentinel over buried treasure, but show a surprising turn of speed at the threat of

robbery. Others become airborne at the behest of the most curious of agencies.

– THE DEVIL'S STONY COUNTENANCE –

The Devil would often show his displeasure by using stones as missiles, particularly if he felt that his power was being challenged.

Just to keep in practice, he would sit on Winsford Hill in the south of Exmoor and throw stones at its highest point, Dunkery Beacon. It being the highest point in Somerset, and consequently the closest to Heaven, he nursed a particular hatred for that spot. On its top you can still see those stones that landed there to mark his anger. One day, however, failing to take a certain stone's weight into account, he misjudged his throw. Being made of flint it was heavier than the others, and fell short of the beacon, landing near the River Quarme.

Furious with the stone for having let him down, the Devil cursed it. Since it had shown such a yearning for the river it is not allowed to rest like other stones, but is compelled to go down to the waters and drink every morning at the sound of the first cock crow. Perhaps the stone on nearby Monkham Hill was the source of a similar disappointment, for that one too is compelled to drink at a spring whenever it hears the clock strike in Dunster.

– THE DEVIL AND CHEDDAR GORGE –
ANOTHER UNFINISHED MASTERPIECE

As well as throwing stones, the Devil's spite gives rise to the kind of strength that enables him to dig through solid rock. This is how the Cheddar Gorge was created – as a result of jealousy, malice and showing off.

Although few of the ancient Giant race then remained, the results of their labours could be seen littered all over the landscape: strange rock formations, stone circles, and the enormous banks, ditches and mounds that have been so wrongly attributed by historians and archaeologists to human building skills. They served to remind the Devil of superhuman powers that could be said to rival his own.

The Devil decided to outdo them all. He started to dig in the Mendip Hills, creating a great gash in the Earth, the deepest and longest and most spectacular in Britain. Quite soon his spadework had almost reached all the way down to an underground river, the Cheddar Yeo, so he then decided to put the trench to good use as a water-course. By diverting the River Axe and releasing the torrent of the Yeo from its subterranean prison, he intended to drown any settlements south of the gorge, along with their puny inhabitants.

He was almost successful in this endeavour – he had dug down over 440ft, and you can see where the River Axe flows at the bottom of the gorge. However, the violent surge of the underground water is still trapped because – fortunately for human survival in the region – the Devil was distracted. 'So fickle as wanton woman,' as the local inhabitants might have said, with a sigh of relief …

What had grabbed Old Nick's attention was another stone shoveller, who seemed to be even better at it than him: Giant Gorm. The giant, known for his strength rather than his brains, had scooped out the Avon Gorge with just one sweep of his spade. It was the sound of this scraping that had distracted the Devil and so, incensed at the competition, he deserted his efforts to see what was happening.

Raging with jealousy, he terrified poor Gorm – who had just enough sense to dump his spadeful of gouged-out rock rather than attempt to flee whilst still carrying its weight. This created Maes Knoll, a mighty hill whose features were centuries later to be naively credited to the warriors and builders of the Iron Age. Clumsy Gorm still hoped to throw off his ferocious pursuer by making for the sea, and he just managed to reach the Bristol Channel. But, within yards of safety, he fell flat on his face – and by then was too tired to rise. His bones formed Brean Down, a spectacular peninsula that produces its own special wave effect – the 'Silver Stacks' – from billows 20ft high that appear just beyond its tip. His outflung hands formed the islands of Steep and Flat Holm.

Satisfied with having thwarted England's largest giant of the day, the Devil did not feel the need to complete his malicious work at Cheddar, and since then has been resting on his laurels (at least in this respect). Thankfully, the terrible flood of 1968 – during which cars and boulders the size of cars were washed through the gorge – did not remind him to complete the task that he once started, and that nature has so destructively improved upon.

Meanwhile, the gorge and its spectacular caves have been voted Britain's second most popular tourist attraction, rivalled only by the Dan-yr-Ogof caves in Wales. The tiny town of Cheddar that sprang up alongside the River Axe, where the Devil had abandoned his trench, became famous for the world's favourite cheese. Varieties of Cheddar cheese are now produced in several far-flung countries, and cholesterol-watchers and calorie-counters would say that the Devil's work thereby continues to this day.

Tourists marvel at the passages and caverns beneath Cheddar's towering limestone cliffs, at the chambers lined with extraordinary stalactites, and the many wonders still to be discovered. They are also told that this labyrinth of tunnels and pathways is the by-product of cheese mining. Should any doubt this, huge racks with layer upon layer of enormous cheeses can always be seen maturing in the caves.

Above ground, Cheddar's cliffs are very popular with walkers, climbers, wildlife enthusiasts and botanists. The latter two sometimes come into conflict – as in the 'whodunnit' case of the missing Cheddar whitebeam saplings ...

The unique habitat of the cliffs has produced species found nowhere else in the world, including three new kinds of whitebeam discovered as recently as 2009. In the past, Cheddar's own unique breed of sheep had grazed the area, producing the ideal conditions in which these botanical rarities, and many others, could evolve and thrive – but by 1970 the sheep had died out.

In order to keep the area grazed in the manner to which it had become accustomed, replacements had to be found. Thus the south side of the gorge, which belongs to Lord Bath's Longleat estate, introduced goats (not known as fussy eaters) to fulfil this function. Meanwhile the north side, owned by the National Trust, has seen the recent introduction of Soay sheep, Neolithic survivors from the most remote Hebridean islands and well known for their adaptability.

These rarest of trees have consequently been decimated, but no one can decide whether the sheep or the goats are the culprits. So shaggy and shy are these creatures that most mortals can't tell them apart, and so, in contrast to their biblical forebears, blame may yet be apportioned to both.

⁓ THE DEVIL TURNS TO BUILDING ⁓

Although the Devil would never have admitted to imitating the industrious endeavours of humans, it was he who made the Tarr Steps at one of Exmoor's most popular beauty spots.

Known locally as the Devil's Bridge, they span the River Barle. Given that evil does not like to cross running water, it must have been a brave undertaking. A hopeful one too, as its purpose was to provide the Devil with a suitable place for sunbathing – thus revealing an optimism to which other locals have never aspired, given that Exmoor is one of the wettest places in England.

The Devil brought the stones to the River Barle in his apron. This one had reinforced apron strings, as previous attempts at carrying stones had failed when the strings broke. These earlier efforts had been carried out in order to dam the rivers nearest the churches and thus drown the pious, but he had been so enthusiastic and hasty that he had often filled his apron beyond capacity. The tumbled heaps of stones found all over Exmoor still serve to remind people of his failed attempts – to others they are mere geology.

The materials having been successfully assembled, the stone bridge was completed – with its elegant lines eclipsing many a church in style, and looking rather like an extra large, rust-free sun-lounger. Its creator was of course not prepared to share it with any of the local riff-raff, who would certainly have benefited from such a structure to take them safely over that rapid river. To make sure that he never needed to share, he laid a curse on whoever first dared to cross it.

It wasn't long before the locals had come up with a plan (this is where animal lovers should look away or go and make a cup of tea); with their priest on standby, they sent a cat across the bridge. A thunderbolt shot down from the sky and turned the cat into a fireball. There was a shriek, a terrible smell of burnt fur, and moggy was no more.

With the Devil so publicly wrong-footed, the priest seized the moment and rushed onto the bridge where the furious Devil had appeared. There they had the most vehement of

verbal confrontations. It would seem that the priest drew on
the Old Testament rather than the New for his inspiration
throughout, as his imprecations turned the river to steam,
made the banks spew out stones, the trees wither like grass in a
drought and passing pigeons fall dead from the sky.

The Devil was defeated and slunk away with his barbed tail
between his legs, leaving the bridge for pack-horse drivers,
walkers, deer stalkers, tourists and all other mortals to enjoy.

~ THE WEDDING AT STANTON DREW ~

It was Midsummer's Day, an auspicious day for a wedding,
and the June sunlight seemed as though it would shine forever.
After the ceremony and the feast, the bride wanted the dancing
to happen in the open air: 'Not in that gurt, dark, stuffy ol'
barn,' she said.

So the revellers went out into one of her father's fields, followed by the best fiddler to be found in all the country round

about. Dance followed dance, and in that warm evening sun-
shine the cider firkins were emptied as soon as they were filled,
and still the dancing went on. At last the sun set on that long
and happy day, and the full moon rose to partner the dancers
with its blossoming silver light, whilst their feet still trod the
lingering streaks of copper from the west. So bright was the
moon that the wedding party were still dancing unawares into
the night – until the music suddenly stopped.

''Tis the Sabbath and I'll play no more,' said the fiddler.

'But 'tis my wedding!' shrieked the outraged bride.

'Even if it be the Queen of Sheba's wedding, 'tis still the
Sabbath and I'll not play for'un, and whether you be bride or
groom or guest you should cease your frolickings like good
Christian folk.'

''Tis my wedding and I'll dance if I've a mind to!'

'Then you'll be dancing without music for I'll play no more.'

The fiddler packed his instrument away and stomped off.
His silhouette was soon swallowed by the shadow of the hedge
and for some moments the guests were in disarray, with no one
wanting to be the first to leave. Just as the party felt well and
truly over, another figure stepped into the moonlight.

'Many find my music sweet. I will play for you, Madam, if
you wish,' he said.

The bride looked up at this distinguished stranger. His pale
skin seemed to soak up the silver light until all was turned to
shadows around him, and his eyes were even darker than the
darkest of those. She clapped her hands with glee.

'Play on, play on stranger, and you will be well rewarded.'

'I do not doubt it,' and the eyes darkened around his gleaming smile.

On his way back to the village inn, the first fiddler heard the
sweetest sounds of a violin coming from the place he had just
left. Hardly believing his own ears, he crept back and peered

through a gap in the hedge. Never had he listened to such enchanting music; surely he would have heard of such a player in the neighbourhood. Spellbound, he watched and listened …

Tune slipped into tune and the dancers never missed a step, nor the fiddler a note. Revellers and player were as tireless as each other and soon the short night was almost over. Whilst the music dipped and soared and eager feet trampled the dew, the wedding party did not notice the sky turning paler.

In the grey before the dawn, the fiddler imperceptibly slowed his playing; quite unawares, the dancers gradually slowed their pace in keeping with the music. As their tread slowed, so their feet seemed to become heavier. Indeed it was only with diffi-culty that they could move their limbs at all. Slower still played their musician, until nobody could take a further step and their swaying bodies strived in vain to move from where they stood. Every part of them felt stiff and heavy and bone cold. Stone cold. Even if they could still feel the chill, they could no longer shiver, as what had been flesh and bone was turning into stone. The bride's cry of horror never left her throat, and her bright eyes were filled with the greys of that early morning before they filmed over, and she saw no more.

A good night's work done, the Devil tucked his fiddle beneath his tailcoat and disappeared.

In the clear light of morning, the local fiddler roused the village to see what had become of the wedding party. Where there had been a grassy field, a circle of stones had sprung up overnight. He told the amazed villagers how he had warned against dancing on the Sabbath; he told them what he had then heard and seen. All agreed it would take a better fiddler than the Devil to undo the spell and play stone back into flesh, and that person has never been found.

The first fiddler was a righteous man, but he was not without feelings, and he felt truly sorry at the fate that had befallen the young couple, their family and friends.

The next year, on the anniversary of that fateful party, he rose with the early dawn of Midsummer's Day. He made his way to the field where the circle of stones stood and went to the hedgerow where he had hidden. There he found the dog roses in full bloom and he gently unwound some of their strands from amongst the hawthorn branches and ivy stems. Kneeling in the damp grass, he wove them into a delicate wreath which he placed at the foot of one of the stones which was now known as 'the bride'. He noticed that, as the tiny thorns scraped against the stone, a few drops of blood trickled onto the grass, and his own tears mingled with the dew.

> There are who may this tale esteem
> As some crazed poet's idle dream.
> Yet 'tis not so, I only tell
> What once, tradition says, befell
> In ages past. But, false or true,
> The stones remain in Stanton Drew

BIBLIOGRAPHY

Briggs, Katherine, *A Dictionary of British Folk Tales*, Routledge and Kegan Paul, 1971

Caine, Mary, *The Glastonbury Zodiac*, 1978

Cary, W.M., *Some Ballad/Legends of Somerset*, The Somerset Folk Series No. 14, Somerset Folk Press, 1924

Evans, Roger, *Blame it on the Vicar*, 2006

Floss, Michael, ed., *Folk Tales of the British Isles*, Book Club Associates, 1977

Garton, J.A., *Glowing Embers from a Somerset Hearth*, no publisher, donated to Kennedy-Grant Memorial Library by the Kennedy family

Gibbs, Ray, *Somerset Places and Legends*, Llanerch Publishers, 1991

_____ *The Legendary XII Hides of Glastonbury*, Llanerch Publishers, 1998

Grinsell, L.V., *The Folklore of Stanton Drew, West Country Folklore* No. 5, The Toucan Press, 1973

Hariott Wood, Frances, *Tales of the Polden Hills*, The Somerset Folk Series No. 8, Somerset Folk Press, 1922

Hartland, E.S., ed., *English Fairy and Other Folk Tales*, The Camelot Series

Hurley, Jack, *Legends of Exmoor*, The Exmoor Press, 1973

Lawrence, Berta, *Somerset Legends*, David & Charles, 1973

Leitch, Yuri, *Gwyn*, The Temple Publications, 2007

Mee, A., ed., *Somerset*, Hodder and Stoughton, 1941

Norman, W.H., *Legends and Folklore of Watchet*, 1992

_____ Tales of Watchet Harbour, 1985

Norris, Sally, *Tales of Old Somerset*, 1989

Page, John Lloyd Warden, *An Exploration of Exmoor and the Hill Country of West Somerset*, New York Public Library Collection, 1890

Palmer, Kingsley, *The Folklore of Somerset*, 1976

Phillips, Beryl, *A Short History of Drayton and its Environs*, no publisher, 2000

Read, John, *Cluster O'Vive: Stories and Studies of Old World Wessex*, Somerset Folk Press, 1923

Rhodes, M.B., *Songs and Stories of Ruth Tongue*, Halsway Manor Society, 2009

Sutherland, Patrick and Nicolson, Adam, *Wetland Life in the Somerset Levels*, Michael Joseph Ltd, 1986

Taylor, R., *The Wonders of Nature and Art*, 1780

Tongue, Ruth, *The Chime Child*, Routledge and Kegan Paul, 1967

_____ *Somerset Folkore*, The Folklore Society, 1965

_____ *Forgotten Folk Tales of the English Counties*, Routledge and Kegan Paul, 1970

Westwood and Simpson, *The Lore of the Land*, Penguin, 2005

Wood, John, *A Description of Bath, 1765*, self-published, 1765

Wright, Brian, *Somerset Dragons*, Tempus Publishing Ltd, 2002